I was born in Somerset, but spent most of my life in West Yorkshire.
In late 2004, my American wife and I decided to move to Norfolk. We married in 1976.

After an injury, my father became an unemployed gardener for Eleven years, until younger men were taken into the armed forces. Most of that time, we lived in poverty, in a small hamlet a mile away from all the villages.

A nervous breakdown kept me off school a year, after which I passed a scholarship for the Grammar School. Later, further problems made me leave without any qualifications to go to agriculture and regain my health. I spent twenty-five years in farming and twenty-five in private gardening.

I always loved nature, especially birds, and still do.

My hobby of oil painting landscapes resulted in a reasonable number of sales. Writing rhyming poetry and small non-fiction booklets was also successful, and now I am testing my luck with the longer stories.

'The Boy From Harker's Bridge' could be said to be my life up to having to drop education; the later part might be my dreams of what might have been.

ISBN: 978-1-84944-066-0

British Library Cataloguing in Publication Data.
A catalogue record for this book is available from the British Library.

Published by UKUnpublished

UKUnpublished
.CO.UK

www.ukunpublished.co.uk
info@ukunpublished.co.uk

THE BOY FROM HARKER'S BRIDGE

By

Mervyn S. Whale

CHAPTER 1

"Hello, boys. Why are you so late, George? I was getting worried, and was about to come up the hill to look for you."

The speaker was Mrs. Gwen Briggs, a slim dark-haired woman of about thirty-eight. Like most of the people who lived in the valley her clothes were plain and well worn. The two boys also wore garments that had seen better days, but they were clean. In the case of Alec's short pants they had been neatly patched on the seat. This wasn't surprising because he was the third boy to have worn them. Gwen's friend's son was the first, then George. When Alec had finished with them they'd go into the ragbag for either patching something else or to be cut up for a tab rug.

"It wasn't our fault, Mum," George said. "Wilfred Baker has a metal lunch box and he hits people with the corner of it. It hurts, and he did it to Alec. I was able to get it off him and I threw it over the wall into a field so that he couldn't get it in time to hit him again. Just then Mrs. Baker came and dragged me to the gate and made me fetch it."

"Did she? Just wait until I see her."

"She's coming now." George indicated where a tall heavily built woman was walking quickly up the earthen track that acted as a street. She wore a blue overall, and had an angry look on her face as she halted in front of Gwen.

"You'd better make your kids leave my boy alone," she snarled. "I had to get his lunch box out of a field because your brats threw it over the wall and he couldn't climb over."

"Just a moment, Jean. Have you asked your wonderful Wilfred why it was thrown over? And my boys are not brats."

"He did it because they're brats and bullies, and he knew there were two of them."

"Bullies? Wilfred is two years older than George, and Alec's only seven. He's much bigger than George. He's the bully, going around hitting younger ones with that box. George threw it over because he'd hit Alec, so that he couldn't do it again. Another thing, don't ever dare to lay a finger on either of my boys again or you'll be in dire trouble.

"If you think that you've a complaint come to William or myself, but keep your hands off them. If you want to grab a boy do it to your horrid son. You had me worried when you made them late like that. I thought they might be hurt, and they'd done nothing wrong." She turned to the boys, "Come inside before I get really angry, and if she or Wilfred ever touch either of you again tell me or your father."

She ushered them inside the cottage where she soon had their teas ready for them. She placed their Coronation mugs, given to all children at King George V1's accession, on the table. This was in the centre of the room so that their father would not hit his head on the glass globe over the gas mantle, as it was a very low ceiling. On the stone flags of the only room on the ground floor were home made tab rugs. By the fire were two easy chairs, and at the table were four lighter ones. All were very old as was all the furniture, but everything was as clean as possible in a dwelling with only a cold tap and a couple of gas rings.

A chest of drawers stood opposite the window. On top of it were bookshelves made from orange boxes. These were for the parents' books; other similar ones held those of the boys but were stacked at floor level where they could reach them.

She was angry because her boys had been called brats and bullies. They did sometimes get into mischief as all children do, but George was probably the quietest child in the school. Though he saw other boys with things he knew his parents could not afford he wasn't bothered by it. He knew that other men in the valley were unemployed. He didn't yearn for a bike he knew would be of little use on the rutted track they called a lane in the hamlet of Harker's Bridge.

The cottages had been built for the workers at Albert Harker's little mill about eighty years ago, and a bridge that gave the place its name was built at the same time for other workers to be able to come from Cullerton, a nearby village.

Anyone wanting to get to that village on anything wider than a horse had to go the long way round.

George preferred to spend his time in the nearby woods and fields watching the birds and animals that lived there. He also liked to go to the local farm and help Sarah Driver with the hens. She was a lot older than her brother, and appreciated the help George gave her at the weekends. They lived in huts scattered around the fields and had to be fed twice every day.

Just as the boys were finishing the meal their father came home after an attempt to obtain work. He'd heard that a plumber was needed and had tried to get the job. He was of medium height with a reddish moustache and jet black hair. After hanging his flat cap on a nail behind the door he went to one of the chairs by the fireside and sat down.

"No luck, love," he replied to Gwen's query. "I'd have done more good in the garden, or fetching firewood. There'll be a lot of newly fallen stuff after the storm last night."

"Never mind, dear, we're all well, and have enough to eat at present. Thanks to Enid we also have enough clothes to keep us warm, even though they're not new. I'm glad I learned needlework at school. The worst things we've to put up with are Jean Baker and her son."

"Why, what have they been doing?"

Gwen explained what had happened. William was angry, but didn't intend to do anything himself unless there was another incident. After spending a short time with their father the boys went out to play. It was a beautiful evening and they soon found other children with whom they began a game of hide and seek in the woods. That lasted until some of them were called home for a wash and bedtime.

When the boys came home in answer to their father's call they found their mother sitting knitting socks on four needles. Much of her spare time she spent making things for the family and the home. Fortunately she liked that kind of work.

She arose and supervised the boys' washing, and gave them glasses of milk and a biscuit each before they went upstairs to the bed they shared. There were only two bedrooms, and they were too small for two beds in the one room, even if they could have been afforded.

Gwen dealt with the feeding and clothing of them all, and William grew vegetables and salads on a small plot of land that belonged to the cottage. He also kept the woodpile well stacked to save buying coal. There was often a toy to be repaired, sometimes with a piece of wire that he'd found on the roads. He also repaired all the footwear when it needed it. Twice each week he went to the Labour Exchange to see if there was a job, and to prove that he qualified for unemployment money. Whilst he was in town he visited the public library and read the newspapers and borrowed books to read at home. He was reading one of them as Gwen re-settled in the chair and picked up her knitting.

"Why did they turn you down, William?" she asked. "Did they give you a reason?"

"Yes, the usual one, I'm too old. I don't think I'll ever get a proper job again. Every boss wants young lads who can go faster and know nothing."

"It's a shame. You've over twenty years of experience and they throw you on the scrap heap just because you had an accident and couldn't work for a few weeks."

"We're all in the same boat, Gwen. I meet fellows from all trades when I go to sign on, and if they are over forty they don't get set on. I met a monumental mason last week who'd been restoring old buildings in charge of six men. A stone slipped and broke his leg. Before the bone was set some young kid had his job. You don't learn those skills in a three year apprenticeship, but he can't get a job putting new names on old gravestones now."

"It isn't your fault so don't worry about it. We're just managing, thanks to Enid providing so much clothing and other things. I see children wearing rags that should have gone into the bag long since. If the women would only use a needle occasionally it would save their kids a lot of shame."

"Yes, and living by the wood saves us a lot of money, but it's hard on you having to do the housework without modern equipment. There are many labour saving things on the market now."

"Even if we could afford them they wouldn't be much use without electricity. I can just manage to buy food and other essentials. The rent goes up tuppence a week next month. To the landlord it's not much, but it's the lads' Saturday pennies to us. £1/4/- is not enough for four people. I just wish that we could afford a wireless for the lads. They really like the gramophone, but Alec has difficulty winding it up if George isn't there."

"Yes, our lives are very basic, yet compared with many in Africa and other places we're rich, if what I read in the library is true. Many of their children get no schooling at all."

"I'm glad that doesn't apply here. Our George is very intelligent, and his teacher wants him to sit for the County Minor Scholarship this year. If he passes he'll be able to go to the Grammar School with no fees to pay."

"How would we afford it, Gwen? He may get free education, but there'd be travelling expenses. Besides, he couldn't go there in hand-me-downs. He'd be sitting with sons of doctors, dentists, bank managers and others. Apart from the shame, he'd feel that his classmates wouldn't want to know him."

"It's not like that. If he passed the exam he'd get a travel pass, and for people like us there are vouchers for clothing and other items as they come up. The school books are provided free. If he got there it could provide him with an opportunity for a better life than this."

"If all that is true perhaps we could manage to send him, but don't say anything to him yet. I'll go to see the headmaster and find out if that's how it works. If it isn't there's no point in him sitting the exam. Now it's getting late, so I think we ought to go to bed."

CHAPTER 2

The next couple of weeks went by as usual with William collecting and cutting up wood for winter and tending the growing vegetables. Gwen was washing, cooking and cleaning with the primitive equipment that could be used in a home without electricity.

There was no further trouble with the Baker family at this time, so perhaps Joe had told his son to leave the boys alone. William was cutting up logs with a hand saw one morning when a black car came into the valley and stopped outside the Briggs home. As the driver got out he spoke to the plumber.

"That's warm work, Bill."

"Yes, it's one of the beauties of burning fallen timber. It warms me when I fetch it, again when I cut it up, and all of us when we burn it, and of course it's free, which is important here. What brings Frank Dobson to Harker's Bridge? You aren't going to spoil the place by building more houses here are you?"

"No, I've come to see you. Are you still unemployed?"

William looked at the visitor more closely. He saw a well built man in his forties with the ruddy complexion of the outdoor worker. He wore a pair of sturdy trousers and a chequered shirt open at the neck, with heavy boots on his feet.

"Yes, and I think that I will be for a long time if there's no improvement. Younger men than me are being put on the dole now. This lack of jobs is hitting a lot of people."

"I'd have come for you a long time ago, but as you know most of my work is on the other side of Bradford. You'd spend half of your wage travelling, and your family would only see you on Sundays. Now I've a contract right here in your own territory. The new chap who's bought the Hill Top Inn is called

Nigel Holdsworth. I know him well as he comes from near Wike, right in my normal stamping ground. He's a forward looking fellow, and he's decided to expand the pub to be a sort of social meeting place with rooms for guests.

"He's going to build a large hall fit for dances, concerts, meetings of all kinds. It will be alcohol free except for champagne at weddings for the toasts, but he'll add another bar close to it so that Dad can slip out for a quick pint whilst Mum looks after the kids."

"That sounds a good idea, just what's needed here."

"He's going to put four bedrooms over the hall in the hope of filling them with whoever will pay for them. I've got the contract to build the extension. I'll need a good plumber, so I'm here to engage the best I know. As I say he's a forward thinking fellow, and he's going to put in one bathroom, and toilets and wash bowls in all the bedrooms. He says that will be the standard that visitors will want in a few years time. I hope that Hitler fellow in Germany won't cause trouble and spoil it for him, but in any case we've got the job.

"There'll be toilets for both sexes at the hall, and a small kitchen for making tea and coffee. The job won't last for ever, but it'll keep you busy for quite some time. You'll need a labourer with you, but that'll come when it's needed. You never know, this contract may bring others in the district, and if it does you'll get the first chance to be the plumber. Will you take it?"

"Of course. When can I start?"

"We'll not be building toilets and such just yet, but if you're willing to do something else you can start tomorrow. I need a good invoice clerk to check what's being delivered. We've men levelling the ground and digging the foundations, but I need that clerk. There are stone, bricks, cement and other things coming in daily. We have a storeman, Fred Binns, but as things get going he'll be busy without having to receive and check deliveries.

"If you've a problem he'll be able to help you. I don't expect you to count the bricks, but if half a dozen wash bowls come in make sure that one hasn't left the wagon before it got there. When the first bit of lead goes in you'll put it there, and I'll find another clerk. You get full plumbers pay from tomorrow. How does all that sound?"

"Wonderful, after nearly four years on the shelf. What time do I start?"

"Eight o'clock, and we usually work until 5.30, unless we stay over in the evening. One hour for lunch."

"Thank you, Frank. I was beginning to wonder if I'd ever get a real job again."

Next morning William, or Bill as his workmates would call him, arrived early at the site. It only took him a quarter of an hour to walk to the pub, so there were no bus fares to pay. He had to inform the Labour Exchange that he'd found work, and later he'd have to collect the final payment due to him. He arranged with Frank to have time off to conform with the rules. Once that was dealt with he worked as many hours as he could. When there was overtime work he took it. He was determined to earn as much money as he could whilst the job was there, as he couldn't forecast how long it would last.

Gwen was delighted when he handed her the first wage packet. "I can scarcely believe this is true," she told him. "After all those years it seems marvellous to have a decent amount of money. We need to use it wisely and try to put a little away each week for when the building is finished. Meanwhile Alec needs new boots at once. I don't think that even you could mend them again."

William gave her the wages untouched. Most of the other men went into the bar after work on pay day, but William went straight home.

"Aren't you coming for a drink, Bill?" Fred asked one Friday. "Most of us do for a while. It's a bit matey, you know."

"Yes, maybe it is, Fred, but my kids need new clothing and shoes and my wife wants new equipment. It's bad enough not having electricity without having to use worn out tools."

"I understand, Bill," Fred said. "Many of us have been in the same boat, but you've had a long dose of it. Nobody will criticise you for looking after your family."

William had found Fred Binns a pleasant person to work with. He was a heavily built man in his fifties. His fair hair was neatly combed, and he had a ruddy complexion. Like all the men he wore clothes made to last as he handled many items that were rough and sharp.

At first William hadn't a lot of work to do. A few loads of sand, stone and other things arrived but only after a couple of weeks did things get busier for him, so he helped Fred or anyone who could use him. He suspected that Frank had made a job for him before there was a need in order to help a good plumber who was in dire circumstances. Gradually doors, bags of nails and other items began to appear, and one day he received a considerable amount of lead piping of various sizes.

"Now I know that I'll be a plumber again," he told Fred. "They may even bring me some taps yet."

"I'm glad for you," the storeman replied. "My brother has no work at present, but he lives in Oldham and there doesn't seem to be anything there at all. If he comes to Bradford Frank will try to help him, but where he is its hopeless."

+ + +

"William, can you be at the school at 7.30 on Wednesday evening to meet Mr. Pighills?" Gwen asked one day.

George was working on a jigsaw, and his brother was sketching on some drawing paper that he'd been given by his teacher.

"Yes, I don't see any reason why I can't. I finish work at 5.30, get home and washed by six. We have our meal and I walk up there. Will you be coming?"

"No, I'll stay here with the boys. Helen offered to come in, but I see no need. You are aware of what we want to know, and now you're working it gives us more hope of his being able to go."

"Don't count too much on my job. If he goes to the Grammar School it will be for several years, and if he went to university it would be a few years more, but we don't have to think about that yet. Even grammar school education will give him a better chance of a decent job, so we'll see what Mr. Pighills says."

The headmaster was very pleased to see that William had made the effort to come to discuss his son's future. He wasn't a tall man, and William guessed his age to be about fifty-five. He wore a smart brown suit and rimless spectacles.

"I'm glad that you've come," he said. "Your wife told me that you've found employment at last, so I wondered if you'd be able to get away to see me. Education is so important and George is such an intelligent boy that he should be given every opportunity. Don't quote me to others, but he's the most intelligent boy in his class, if not in the whole school."

"His mother and I want him to have the best, and Alec too when his turn comes, William said. My chief concern is finance. My wife said that there are grants for travel, but it doesn't end there. I've had no work for nearly four years until recently and this job won't last for ever. I wouldn't want our son to be embarrassed because he was seen by the other boys as inferior. Children can be mean and hurtful.

"He must seem worthy to be with them, he'll be judged by the sons of the rich according to the clothes he wears. George is a very sensitive boy and would be hurt badly if the boy sitting next to him treated him as unwanted. How could he benefit from the school if he felt permanently embarrassed?"

Mr. Pighills listened to William's anxieties attentively until he had finished. He had a distinguished air about him that made people respect his comments and opinions. His greying hair, thin on top and combed neatly from front to back, and his kindly smile added to the whole impression of a teacher who could be trusted to give worthwhile advice and have the welfare of the pupil foremost in his mind.

"Don't worry, Mr. Briggs," he said. "There are clothing grants for those who genuinely cannot afford to buy school uniforms and sports equipment such as football boots. Although you're working now I don't think that you'd have any trouble getting a grant for the first year. I'll personally promise this, if the authorities don't give the help I will, from my own pocket.

"This may sound like charity and I suppose it is, but it's also for the benefit of this school and its staff. If we provide a star pupil it gets this school a good record. I know a school not very far away that hasn't sent any child to any secondary school, either grammar, art or technical college in the last five years. We expect to do much better than that this year, and we sent three last year. All I ask is that you don't mention my offer to anyone."

"I'll say nothing, and neither will my wife. He still has to pass the exam before that problem comes up."

"I don't think that there'll be any difficulty there, though it can happen that a really bright pupil will get nerves and lose it. We must get his application in as soon as possible."

"Thank you for taking part of your evening to see me," William said, "and for having such an interest in my son's future."

+ + +

"George," his father said a couple of evenings later, "how would you like to sit for the County Minor Scholarship? If you pass you'll be able to go to the Grammar School and have a much better education. That in turn will give you a hope of a really good job, and no struggle like we've had in recent years."

"I'd like it very much, Dad, but Grammar School is only for the rich and a few really brainy ones. Mr. Pighills said on Friday that only the very cleverest would be allowed even to sit for the exam."

"Well you're the top of the class aren't you? Mr. Pighills especially wants you to sit, because he thinks that you'll pass."

"Then I'll try to pass. I know that it's a great chance. One of the older boys who went there a few years ago is now at Leeds University."

"When you get to school tomorrow ask the headmaster to put your name down for it. You may have to bring home a form for me to fill in."

When the list of accepted candidates was issued George Briggs' name was on it, and so was that of his friend, Ronnie Schofield. Alice Shepherd was also on it, so there would be two from the valley out of the seven allowed to try. That meant George would have several friends with whom he could await the start of the exam and spend the lunch break.

A few hundred yards above the cottages the lane divided and the other half of it went directly to the mill, now owned by Mr. Walter Shepherd. His home was at the junction. He didn't own any of the cottages, but both of Wilfred's parents worked at the mill. The Shepherds had one daughter who was in George's class at school, and she had a brother who was several years older than her. She didn't normally join in the activities of the valley as her father wanted her to have friends other than their neighbours.

Jean Baker was angry when she heard that George Briggs was entered to try for the County Minor Scholarship. Her son hadn't been chosen to represent the school in his year.

"How does that brat get to try for the Grammar School when my Wilfred didn't?" she asked her neighbour, Constance Manning. "His father's been out of work for years, so how will they be able to afford it, even if he passes? My Wilfred wasn't even given a chance."

Miss Manning was a tall woman with blonde hair that was brown when it grew out of her head. She claimed to have a good figure, but some would call her thin. She didn't like living in Harker's Bridge, but she was such a trouble maker that her two brothers had told her that unless she lived there, or somewhere equally distant from their wives, she wouldn't get any income from the family business, and as she hated having to go to work she put up with living there.

"Why not?" she asked. "He should have as much opportunity as anyone else."

"The teachers said he wasn't clever enough. They said it would build up his hopes, and when he failed it would be bad for him. How did they know that he'd fail? Were they saying that he's a dunce or a fool? When they are letting that brat sit they are saying that he's cleverer than my son."

"Well that's how it goes around here, Jean. Look at me, I was in this valley long before that Field woman came, but everyone makes a fuss of her. She's as thick as thieves with the Briggs family."

"Oh well, we all know what they are, scroungers with brats."

"It's always the same, Jean. Some can have everything and others have to work hard and have nothing." The Briggs family have been on Public Relief for over three years but their lad can sit. If he passes we'll have to pay for his education. Of course they have friends in high places."

"What do you mean?"

"Look at Helen Field. She's thick with them, and I know that she's pally with Mrs. Pighills. Her mother went to school with Mrs. P. I'll bet that she's got him into the exam."

"Can you prove that?"

"No, I can't prove that she's done it, but I know it's true about her mother."

"What makes me mad, Constance, is the fact that the son of a fellow who hasn't worked for years gets in before our Wilfred, and both Joe and I are at the mill all the time. I know he's up on the building site now, but how long will that last?"

"I think that woman will have a hand in it somewhere. She knows that you are friendly with me, so she may have done it to spite me. She'll gloat over it as she struts up and down, thinking that she's scored over me if it hurts you."

The ill feeling between the two spinsters was well known to all in the valley and many in the nearby villages. When Helen moved into the cottage next door to the Briggs home she tried to be pleasant to everyone, as was her nature. She had no employment, and didn't need any as she had inherited a large sum when her father died. She sold the large house and bought the cottage in the valley near the woods she loved. She said it was worth being without modern conveniences to wake up in the morning hearing the chaffinches and other birds singing.

At first Constance returned her greetings, but when she saw the younger woman becoming popular she became jealous. Her dislike of the quiet hamlet affected her relationship with the people of the valley, and apart from Jean Hudson she had no friends. She stopped speaking to Helen, and when asked why she went indoors and never admitted the other woman's existence again. The only person she hurt was herself as Helen would willingly have accepted the other single woman as her friend. Now the only person she talked with was Jean Baker, and all that woman wanted was someone to listen when she wanted to malign 'those two brats' as she always called them.

The day for the examination arrived and George was rather tense that morning. Probably all were nervous, but he'd more reason than most. The candidates all had to go to a hall in the town where they would attend school if they passed. Gwen had been with her son to find the place, but he had to go without her this time. He was making final preparations for departure when there was a knock on the door. He opened it to find Mr. Shepherd, the mill owner, standing there. He was a man of medium height and rather stocky build. He wore a casual jacket and heavy duty trousers.

"Hello, George," the man said. "I suppose that you're like our Alice this morning, a bundle of nerves about the examination."

"Well, sir, it's rather different from a normal school day, and I'm a bit scared because I've never been so far from home alone before."

"You won't be alone. I hear that there'll be seven from your class."

"Yes, that's true, but some are going on the bus, and my friend Ronnie's going in his father's car. They can't take me because they're having the back seat replaced."

"Would you like to go in my car with Alice?"

"Oh yes please. Is that why you're here? I'll call Mum, she's upstairs."

Mrs. Briggs came downstairs in answer to her son's call. "Thank you, Mr. Shepherd," she said when she knew why he was there. "It's very kind of you to think of George. He's more scared of travelling than of the exam."

"Mrs. Briggs, you have a very bright boy who has good manners and is worth helping. I was talking with Mr. Pighills and he thinks that both your son and my daughter will pass. Everyone knows that you've had bad luck lately as a family. William's working now, but you'll need good friends for a while yet. Neither of you works for me, and as an employer I've to be neutral to all, but I don't think it will hurt me to help the lad to have an even chance. All the others go to town regularly. He hasn't been able to do so. If he goes and returns with Alice it'll take that stress off him, and perhaps it'll help him."

"Thank you again. It'll take a major load off his mind. I offered to travel with him, but he thought it would affect his image with his peers."

"Yes, he was probably right, and his refusal proves that he has enough spirit to face his own problems, but this is the most important day of his life so far. I don't think anyone can object to it if I help a boy when his whole future can be at stake. Are you about ready, George?"

"I'm quite ready, sir."

"Then say 'Goodbye' to your mother, and we'll go tell Alice that she's to ride with a boy. Actually she's the one who suggested it."

"Then I must thank her as well as you, sir. I was a bit scared having to go all that way before the exam."

"You don't have to worry now, and I think that you'll be alright in the test. Mr. Pighills says you and Alice are his star pupils."

As they conversed they walked up to the mill house where Alice was awaiting them. Her mother, a tall slim lady, welcomed George and wished him success, then her husband and the two children climbed into the black Ford that was standing outside the house. When they arrived at the hall where the examination was to take place Mr. Shepherd said a few words of encouragement to them both before they left the car.

"I don't think either of you'll have any difficulty with the exam papers. This test isn't to catch you out, it's for you to show what you know, just as in the classroom. Good luck to both of you. I've a fair idea of when you'll finish, so I'll be waiting near the gates when you come out."

Alice had been very nervous at home, but she'd travelled and mixed with strangers more than George had. Like him she had been trained to be polite and thoughtful for others, and she'd realised that George would have problems with having to travel so far. She'd spoken to her father about it, and her concern for him had eased her own anxiety. She was determined to help him as much as possible before and between the tests. Of course during the examination periods they wouldn't be sitting anywhere near each other.

Each child was allocated a seat in the hall where he or she would be isolated from all others by a few feet, and no two from the same school were to sit near each other. The man in charge issued the first paper and called for complete silence during the tests. Once permission was given to start George looked through all the questions before beginning to write. He didn't think them too hard, and was checking his answers when the order came to put down the pens.

After the answer papers were collected there was a short break before the next subject was given out. Alice and George found their friends and had a refreshing break together. Alice was pleased to see that her companion was completely relaxed, more so than she was, and she was glad they'd been able to take away the problem that would have stressed him before the exam started.

After lunch other papers followed on different subjects, and when all were finished the Cullerton group compared notes. All had some anxiety, but most were fairly confident that they'd a good chance of passing the exam. The hardest part now would be waiting for the results to come through to the school in the near future.

+++

When Mr. Pighills read out the results at a Friday afternoon meeting five had passed including both the Harker's Bridge children. A great cheer went up, but the winners were sorry for the two losers who had suffered the same problems as they had. One of these later passed another examination for a different school.

Both George and Alice realised that their lives would change dramatically from then on. Alice would go to the Girls' Grammar School, so apart from travelling George wouldn't see much of her. They decided it would be a wise move to walk up to the train together each morning, but as either could have days when they came home later and couldn't let the other know they would come home separately. Both the other boys who had passed were George's friends, Ronnie more so than Reggie was.

All agreed that the first thing to do was to enjoy the holiday and forget for the time being the changes in their lives that lay ahead. When the mill closed down for the annual holiday week the Bakers went to Blackpool, as they did every year. Nobody else in the valley went anywhere for more than a day, except the Shepherds. Most of them couldn't afford to do so. With fields and woods so close the children were able to enjoy a healthy holiday, and George had opportunity to watch the birds and spend time on the farm.

CHAPTER 3

Whilst the young people were busy preparing for and taking the examination William continued his work of receiving the goods at the building site. The area was cleared and the foundations were laid. It was not very long before the main pipes for clean water going in and sewage leaving the extension were put in.

As the building grew the time came when another man relieved William of the clerical work, giving him time to do his own job as a plumber, fitting pipes for the first time in nearly four years. This was his trade, and he worked confidently knowing that he was earning money for his family and easing Gwen's burden of poverty. He didn't know how long the job would last, but he worked carefully and made sure that every joint was as near to perfect as he could make it.

Gradually the new section began to rise from its muddy surroundings. The main aim of Frank Dobson was to get the outer walls up and the roof on before the winter set in. Once that part was finished the men would be able to work no matter what the weather was like. Inner walls could be built and floors put in even if there happened to be six feet of snow outside.

Before long William was fitting taps and connecting the various pipes in the small kitchen and new toilets. Plasterers, electricians and gas fitters were following on, but owing to the size of the hall they didn't cause him any problems. A company of bar fitters came to fix the pumps and other things in the new lounge. They brought their own plumber, so William didn't have to attend to anything there. He had enough for the time being getting the hall's environs ready for the team who would follow him. He was given a young lad to help him with the work as lead is very heavy and some parts of the work needed two people.

He had all the ground floor finished before the other people needed to move into the kitchen or toilets. By this time the upper rooms were ready for him. There were four bedrooms and a bathroom. Each bedroom had a wash basin and a toilet, so pipes had to be put in to carry water to and from them. There would be tea making facilities as well, but all that would need was a power plug and that did not concern the plumber. The tea making was an unusual feature in small country hotels and en suite bedrooms were normally found only in the cities. Nigel Holdsworth was far seeing and he decided he only needed one bathroom, but being able to make a drink of tea or coffee and attend to bodily functions in the middle of the night without leaving the room would attract guests.

William attended to the bedrooms first so that the others could follow without him having to rush the work.

"Why don't we do the bathroom first?" his assistant asked. "It's nearest to the lift on that side."

"Yes, Jim, but those electricians and plasterers will move faster once they are up here with lower ceilings than the hall. If we have the bedrooms ready they will have all the fiddly bits to slow them down whilst we do the bathroom. The secret is to always be well ahead of the next team; you can give it more time and do a better job."

One morning Frank and Nigel came to where the plumbers were working. They made an inspection of all the work done so far. Frank stopped to have a few words with William.

"How's it going, Bill? Have you any problems?"

"From your point of view it's fine, from mine it's going too well."

"What do you mean?" Nigel asked. He was a fairly young man for a pub landlord, which was probably why he had ambition and foresight for the extension of the building. His medium brown hair was neatly trimmed, and he was clean-shaven. He wore a blue shirt and grey slacks.

"I don't want it to end," William explained. "I'm not looking forward to another three years of unemployment with joy."

"The pity is that he lives just down the road at Harker's Bridge," Frank explained. "I bring a lot of the men here in an old bus, but for Bill to go to the other side of Bradford every day would be impractical. Almost all my contracts are there. I did hope that this would bring other jobs here, but it hasn't. Winter's here now with dark weather and frosts. With this snow having arrived early there's no chance. Bill's work is nearly finished now. I'll find him something to do for a while, but it'll not be for long I fear. It's a great pity; he's one of my best men."

Nigel stood looking thoughtful for a few minutes, watching William working. "Do you know anything about bar work?" he asked the plumber.

"I've never done it, but I'm willing to learn. I'll do almost anything legal to save Gwen from the poverty we've had. Also George is starting at the Grammar School, and we don't want to be an embarrassment for him. 'What does your father do, Briggs?' 'He's unemployed,' 'Oh really,' and the banker's son and the doctor's son don't want to know him any more."

"Yes, I see what you mean, and that's just how it's likely to be. When we get this section running I'm going to need some more staff. Of course I could use part timers, but if you'd be willing to learn the job, and do other things when needed, I'll give you a job. It won't pay plumber's rate, but I'll guarantee to pay more than the Labour Exchange. You'll also get meals when on duty, and a good barman can earn a decent amount in tips. Do you drink?"

"I can't afford to do."

"I allow half a pint of mild or bitter every time you come on duty. Unlike some employers I don't object to staff having a drink, so long as they keep sober. When I was training for this trade I worked for a man who didn't allow staff to have any drink whilst working. It cost me a lot of money, some customers only tip if they see you pull the drink, or already have one on the bar. That was a high class hotel, and there would have been plenty of tips. I believe in letting staff have a chance to do well for themselves, so long as they are doing well for me and my customer."

"You can trust Bill," Frank said. "He's as honest as they come, and I'm sure he'll not risk his job by having too much." He turned to the plumber, "You must be careful, Bill, as you haven't been drinking you'll not be able to deal with it like most men."

"That's settled then," Nigel said, "As soon as Frank has finished with you come to see me."

"Better than that," Frank suggested, "would be for him to phase out of my employment gradually and do a couple of days a week training with you. That way you'll have a man who knows what he's doing when the hall opens."

"That's a very good idea. It'll be best for everyone. Come to me on Mondays and Tuesdays at first, because they're usually the quietest days. I'll get Percy to teach you the basics. When the new bar opens you'll go on it with Elsie and she can teach you the fancy drinks. How does that sound?"

"I like it," Frank said. "We'll work out how to pay him for his tax record whilst he has two jobs at one place. He'll not have to pay any, but we must make sure that he's safe from any mistakes."

"It's fine by me too," William said. "When do we start this? For whom do I work next Monday?"

"You may as well start in the bar," Frank told him. "You're well ahead of the others, and it'll let you see how you like it. I'm just sorry that I've nothing for you myself."

"In that case I think it best if you come with me to meet your teacher if Frank doesn't object," Nigel said. "We may as well get it all settled now when both Frank and I are here."

Nigel took William into the older part of the building to where a middle aged man with grey hair was drawing beer off from the pumps ready for opening time.

"Percy, can you spare a minute?" Nigel asked.

"Of course," the older man replied. "What can I do for you?"

"I would like you to teach this man how to be a good barman. Not just now, but he's been recommended by Frank Dobson. His work as a plumber is nearly finished, and as Frank has no other contracts this side of Bradford he'll need other employment. We'll need some more staff when the new hall is ready for use, so as he lives near it seemed a good idea to both Frank and me for him to work here two days a week to learn the job."

"How much do you know about bar work?" Percy asked.

"Nothing, but I'm willing to learn anything rather than go unemployed again."

"Right, that's fine. What the boss wants we'll supply." He turned to Nigel, "When will he start?"

"Next Monday and Tuesday, two days a week until Frank's work is completed. If you teach him about the bar and beer, cleaning the pumps and pipes, he'll learn about the fancy drinks when he gets on the other bar with Elsie.

"But that won't be open all week, will it?"

"No, but he can help in here or wherever we need a pair of hands." He looked at William, "I don't expect to need you to make the beds."

"I'd do that rather than go to the Labour Exchange," William replied with a smile."

Nigel stood for a few seconds, then spoke to Percy, "Look, this isn't a scheme to give your job to a younger man. Your job is safe, but William has had a hard time for over three years and he's well known to Frank. I don't want you to be worried by his coming to us."

"Thanks for telling me that, Nigel. In these times anybody nearing sixty wonders how long his job will last. Only last week my brother's firm found a reason to sack him and give his place to a kid of twenty-three. He'd worked for them for thirty years."

"Don't worry, we don't work like that here."

Percy was obviously relieved, and he turned to William with a happier look on his face.

"This job is easy enough. The only problem is the customers. Most are really nice people, but we do get awkward types sometimes. We soon get rid of them, send them to the Fleece or the King's Arms if we can."

On the following Monday William arrived for work at ten o'clock dressed in clean clothes and shoes.

"What time do you call this, Bill?" one of the bricklayers shouted.

"Look at him, he's dressed for a wedding," another worker said. "Are you taking over Frank's job?"

Once they heard that he was to become a barman those who knew of his recent hard luck were pleased for him.

"Just don't pull me short measure," one lad said. "I'll examine my pint very carefully, and don't you dare to connect the pump to a water tap. I never trust plumbers."

William took all the joking in the way that it was given as he went to report to Percy. The bar opened at 11.30, so the first hour was spent in familiarising him with the location of the various kinds of bottled beer, fruit juice and spirits. He also had to learn which glass was used for each drink, and there were quite a collection to choose from.

Nigel came into the bar as Percy was teaching him how to pull a good pint from the pumps. The beer could be returned to the barrel, so he drew three pints and poured them into a bucket. Percy and Nigel were both satisfied by the way he filled the glass.

During the lunch period William had served seven customers he did not know and all seemed satisfied. Then one of the men from the site came into the bar. He wore a thick jersey and well worn trousers decorated with clay. On his head was a cap that had been brown once, but was now faded by sun and rain. There were at least three days' growth of beard on his face and he had a cheery smile. Percy was about to serve him.

"No Percy," he said, "I want that new chap to attend to me. I want to see if he's any good."

William moved up to that end of the bar. "Yes, sir," he enquired, "What can I do for you?"

"You can pull me a pint of mild, and I want a good one. I'm the Dobson Construction Company's tester of beer supplied to our workers."

"Yes, sir, and we all know that you are the expert on the subject. I've heard that Bert Smith is renowned for his knowledge of beer." He placed the glass on the bar, "I do hope you enjoy it, sir."

Percy was highly amused once he realised that the two men were friends. "You handled that well," he said. "Courtesy with control of the situation. I liked it, but you knew him, wait until you get one you don't know."

"You've not made a bad job of the beer either," Bert remarked. "I may come again some day."

"Yes, like today at 5.30 I suppose."

"That could just be possible," Bert agreed. "Now I have an important appointment with a pile of bricks. Don't worry, Bill, you'll make it. They're not all as awkward as me."

The episode with Bert had done a lot to settle William's nerves, which was why the fellow had come into the bar at lunchtime. He normally waited until after work to slake his thirst.

As it was Monday there were very few customers both at lunchtime and in the evening. Tuesday was similar, so the two men had a good chance to get to know each other. At home William found it strange not eating meals with his family, and Gwen was concerned he might not be fed properly. Apart from those minor concerns both were glad that he wouldn't have to return to the unemployment queue.

CHAPTER 4

"Wilfred, stop it!"

The speaker was Doris Slater, a girl of nearly fourteen who lived in the valley with her widowed mother. She was well built with shoulder length black hair and a healthy complexion. She was pleading with the boy who held Alec with one hand as with the other he forced the child's right arm up behind him.

"Why should I? These brats have got me into trouble more than once. Now I've got this one when his mother isn't here, and his brother isn't at our school."

He gave the arm a jerk and Alec cried out in pain. Doris tried to free him, but the older boy jerked the arm again.

"The more you interfere and the worse it'll be for him. What's it to you anyway? He's not your brother."

"No, but his mother has paid me to look after him until she's well again. Please, Wilfred, let him go."

"Not likely, I haven't finished with him yet. I'll make him pay for what his mother and George did to me. They got me into trouble with my dad."

"They only stopped you from hurting me," sobbed Alec.

"Well they aren't here now to stop me."

"No, boy, but I am, and you can be sure that now I'm here you'll let him go."

Wilfred turned and saw a heavily built woman dressed in a green jumper and a medium length brown skirt. Her short brown hair had a reddish tinge in it that caught the sunlight and her features registered anger. Beside her were two small boys wearing knitted jerseys and short grey pants.

"Let go of the boy I say."

"Who are you? What's he to you?"

"I'm Mrs. Donovan, and he's to me a small boy who needs rescuing from a savage brute." She reached out and pulled Wilfred's hands away from Alec. "Now go home. I'll tell Alec's mother when I get to the valley. He's too small for you to torment, you nasty bully."

"Thank you, Mrs. Donovan. He's too strong for me to make him let Alec go," Doris told the woman.

"Where's Alec's mother? She shouldn't send him alone all this way."

"She's at home. She does take him and collect him every day, but she had the flu so she gave me a shilling to look after him this week, but I couldn't stop Wilfred. He's as big as me, and he's a boy. Mrs. Briggs hopes to be able to come next week."

"You did your best. I heard you plead with him and try to help the kid. I'll tell Mrs. Briggs that it wasn't your fault. Tomorrow we'll all go to school and come home together, that'll stop the bullying. If we don't perhaps he'll hurt Sean and Seamus."

"Yes, you're right. He loves hurting those smaller than himself."

The little group continued their journey together. Wilfred was a long way ahead trying to get home in time to tell his story to his mother before Nora got there. When they arrived at the houses Mrs. Donovan went with Doris and Alec to the Briggs home. Gwen heard their voices and came out to greet them.

"Hello," Nora said. "We haven't met, but my husband is Pat, and we've taken the house behind yours. Our name is Donovan, I'm Nora and these twins are Sean and Seamus."

"Hello, I'm pleased to meet you. Hello, boys."

"Hello, Mrs. Briggs," the boys chorused.

"I've come to tell you about your Alec. That big boy, Wilfred, was twisting his arm up his back and really hurting him. Doris was trying to stop him, but he was too strong for her. I'd to actually drag him off."

"Thank you. I normally take him to school since his brother has to leave earlier. Unfortunately I've had a bad dose of flu and haven't been strong enough to walk all that way twice a day. I thought that he'd be safe with Doris; I never thought that Wilfred would start his antics again. We'd trouble with him and his mother before."

"Tomorrow he and Doris must go and return with us, and the same every day until you're well. Is his father at work?"

"Yes. He was unemployed for over three years, but he recently got a job, otherwise he'd have taken Alec."

"Doris was really trying to earn your shilling, she certainly did her best."

"Thank you, Doris, it wasn't your fault."

"I'm sorry that I couldn't stop him."

"Don't worry about it. Go with Mrs. Donovan until I'm well, and she'll see that you are both alright. She'll stop his nasty ways."

Nora was just about to leave when Jean Baker came hurrying up to them.

"I want you," she snarled at the Irish woman. "I don't know who you are and I don't care. Keep your filthy hands off my son in future."

"And what'll you do if I don't? If I see him deliberately hurting any smaller child I'll stop him, so if you don't want me to do that you should do your job and stop him yourself."

"Who are you to interfere with my boy? He doesn't hurt anyone."

"Don't tell me that. I saw him and I'd to drag him off young Alec who was crying with pain. He knew that Mrs. Briggs wasn't there, so he picked on the poor kid."

"That's a lie. My Wilfred is a good boy."

"Yes, and the Irish sea is full of Guiness. Furthermore, nobody calls Nora Donovan a liar. You've been warned."

"Wait until my Joe gets home, he'll sort you out."

"I don't know him and I've never seen him, but not even an Irishman has ever been able to do that, and a few have tried. Don't think that because we're new here you can boss us around. I see where Wilfred gets his evil ways."

There's no doubt that the two women would have continued and perhaps come to blows if Gwen hadn't intervened.

"Stop it, you two. We all have to live in the valley, so why can't we be peaceful? I've told you before, Jean, about Wilfred's cowardly bullying when there are no adults around. If he ever molests Alec again I'll tell Mr. Pighills about the problem."

"Oh well, we all know he'll take your side," Jean replied with a sneer. "He looks after your brats and gets them into the Grammar School, but he wouldn't let my Wilfred try for the exam in his year."

"What do you mean? Mr. Pighills didn't get George into the school. He sat for and passed the examination."

"I suppose he did, but my Wilfred was never allowed to try for it, and he's too old now. But you're in with the right people. Even our boss is on your side. Both Joe and I work for him, but he's never offered us a ride in his car or done anything else except pay us our hard earned wages. I think it's rotten the way you scroungers get all the people with power on your side."

"We're not scroungers, and we don't get special favours. Mr. Shepherd took George to the exam because he was taking Alice. It was just a kindness that any decent person would do for a child who has a stressful day ahead of him."

"Yes, and Mr. Pighills got him into the exam, and I suppose some other blighter passed him and failed another kid to get him in."

"Are you accusing us all of corruption, Jean?"

"Well it speaks for itself. You're as thick as thieves with Helen Field, and Constance says that her mother went to school with Mrs. Pighills."

Gwen turned to Nora, "Mrs. Donovan, You're a witness to what has been said. I hate to do this the first time we meet, but I must formally ask you to remember what you've heard. I'll report this to the authorities. Our George won his place fair and square. She's just accused Mr. and Mrs. Pighills, Helen Field who's my next door neighbour, and us as well as some examiner of fraud. She'll not get away with it."

"I'll remember," Nora told her. "That tirade was uncalled for. If you don't report it your son could suffer for it some day. Now I must go and prepare a meal. Pat'll be home soon, and he'll be hungry. Doris, you and Alec come to my door at half past eight tomorrow morning and we'll all go together."

All that week Doris and Alec walked the mile to school with Nora Donovan and her boys. On the following Monday Gwen felt able to walk the distance, but Nora suggested that they should all go together in case she found that it was too much for her. Everything went well, and the two women liked each other's company. Gwen was able to give Nora information about local shops and other matters as the Donovans had come from Sheffield and knew nothing about the district.

They decided that they'd always go to the school as a group from then on. That meant that if one of the mothers was unable to go her child or children would still be safe. Doris said that she'd like to be part of the group rather than having to walk alone.

Gwen was very upset by the allegations of Jean Baker. She discussed the matter with William who agreed that she should tell Mr. Pighills and seek his guidance. Gwen sought him after school, and Nora waited in case he wanted to hear her version of the matter.

The headmaster was quite perturbed when he heard the accusations. "Leave it with me for the time being," he advised. "I'll interview Mrs. Baker; we can't have rumours like this floating around."

He sent a letter by post to the Bakers seeking an interview with Jean with her husband present. As they both worked a full week including Saturday mornings he was willing to meet them on Saturday afternoon. They were to bring Wilfred with them.

+ + +

"I have been informed that you, Mrs. Baker, think that your son was treated unjustly when he was of an age to perhaps be eligible to sit for the County Minor Scholarship. You are also reported to have said that George Briggs was awarded a scholarship that he didn't deserve."

"Wilfred wasn't allowed to sit for it with his year, yet that layabout's brat wasn't only allowed to, but was encouraged to sit, and it was given to him. Why should it be given to him and my son not allowed to try?"

"There are rules about which children may enter the exam. Your son's record wasn't good enough. Had he given his time here to learning instead of causing trouble he might perhaps have qualified to enter. He wasn't the only one who was too low in the class."

"How dare you say that he's a trouble maker? Wilfred is a very good boy. Has that Briggs woman been saying things about him?"

"No, not about what happens in lesson time. He's the worst behaved child in all the school. She did mention his bullying of her boy on the way home from school, and apparently it wasn't the first time. I want to take this opportunity to demand that you stop his cruelty to those smaller than himself. Times without number we've had to stop him from hurting younger children. He's a bully and a cruel one. You, Wilfred, had better watch out, because I've had enough trouble from you."

"Do you hear that, Joe? He demands that we do what he tells us. Are you going to be dictated to like that?"

Joe Baker was nowhere near as tall as his wife. He was slimly built and his manner of speaking was much quieter than hers. He looked very unhappy as he heard his wife and the teacher. It was easy for an observer to see that Jean was the dominant partner in the marriage.

"Perhaps he does things when we aren't there that seem bad to Mr. Pighills," he said quietly.

"Rubbish. You may take his side, but I won't listen to this about our son."

Mrs. Baker," interposed the teacher forcibly, "you'll listen to that and a lot more. I didn't just call you here about bullying, though that's bad enough. The other is a far more serious matter and you'll do well to hear my words."

"More serious?" Joe questioned. "What do you mean?"

"I mean your wife's false accusations against me, my wife, the Briggs family and their neighbour, the examiner and perhaps others I don't know about. That is far more serious than bullying."

"I know nothing of this," Joe told him.

"Well I do, and there's an adult witness who heard all of it. If I don't get a written apology addressed to me, and including all those I've mentioned, I'll have no other option than to report the matter to a higher authority. They will examine the veracity of the allegations and when they're proved false your wife will be in dire trouble. The careers of the examiner and myself and the characters of the others are at stake. I want that apology on my desk by Wednesday morning or I'll proceed further."

"I'll not apologise for what's true," Jean stormed.

"If it isn't there by Wednesday you'll live to regret it. False accusations of corruption carry heavy penalties, and rightly so."

"What are you going to do, take me to court?"

"Probably."

"Good. Then all the truth will come out about how you stopped our boy from having a good future and handed it on a plate to that layabout's brat."

"Steady, Jean, we don't want a court case," Joe said with an anxious look on his face. "You can't prove that there was anything illegal."

"I'll try. Now I'm going home, I've wasted enough of my Saturday. Are you coming?"

She stormed out of the school with Wilfred and after saying 'Goodbye' to Mr. Pighills Joe followed her. The teacher locked up the school and walked home with a troubled mind. He knew that there was no corruption and that George had earned his scholarship. He also knew that Jean must be stopped. Her silly jealous attack wouldn't hurt him or any other adult, but it would be distressing for George and could put a question mark in his records for the future. She definitely must be stopped, but he couldn't see how if she didn't write that letter.

When he arrived home he told his wife about the meeting. The lady looked shocked. She wasn't used to such behaviour in an adult. Her father had been a Methodist minister and her upbringing had been peaceful and refined. She still bore the result of that in her character and dignity. Her manner of dress and her kindly facial features all spoke of what she was, a sweet natured lady who would never knowingly hurt anything.

"How did it end then? Did you get her to apologise for her accusations?"

"Unfortunately no. Her husband tried to keep things reasonable, but she completely refuses to admit that she's wrong. According to her that boy of theirs is a perfect saint. She'll hear nothing against him, whereas he's the cruellest bully I've ever known."

"What will happen now?"

"I've told her that I must have a written apology on my desk by Wednesday but she refuses to write one. She wants to go to court where she says all will come out. It will, that she's a fool, but it could be hurtful to young George who's a nice lad, the opposite of Wilfred. I'm hoping that Joe will get her to see sense."

After the evening meal the teacher and his wife made preparations to go to a nearby village to attend a charity concert. They got there just in time for the beginning of it. During the interval they saw Walter Shepherd with his wife and daughter.

"Hello, Walter," he greeted the mill owner. "Hello, Ruth. How do you like your new school, Alice?"

"It's very nice, sir. I'm just getting to know the routine, and some of the other girls."

"She has to get out of bed earlier now," her mother told him. "The train won't wait for her, and she has to be at the bridge on time as she walks up to the station with George Briggs. I'm pleased that they have made that arrangement as it's a long way on a cold morning."

"Is George liking it at his school? Does he say anything?"

"He's really happy. He doesn't like rugby, he's too gentle for rough games, but everything else seems to be just right for him so far. The only thing that worries him is this suggestion that he got his scholarship unfairly. I don't think he could ever be a cheat, he's such a nice boy."

"Hey, we'll have to watch you two," her father laughed. "You're too young to run off to Gretna Green you know."

"Don't be daft, Dad, on our spending money we can't afford the fare," Alice said with a laugh.

"It's good to hear that you're both settling in to what can be the best part of your lives," Mr. Pighills told her. "Now, ladies, I want a word with Walter if you don't mind."

"You'll have to hurry, Charles," his wife told him. "The concert is about to start again."

"In that case I'd like a few words after the National Anthem if you can spare the time, Walter."

"Very well, we'll meet here."

When the concert ended they all met in the foyer. The ladies separated to have a feminine chat whilst the men found a quiet corner.

"Now what can I help you with, Charles?"

"I've a very nasty situation to deal with, and I don't know how to handle it. It concerns the matter your Alice mentioned. Do you know Mrs. Jean Baker?"

"Yes, both she and her husband work for me in the mill."

"In that case perhaps it would be unfair for me to ask your advice."

"Why not tell me what your problem is and let me decide? If I feel that I shouldn't be involved I'll tell you."

"Alright, it's about their son Wilfred and his cruel bullying of younger ones. I know that's true because I've had to deal with him more than once at school. Since George went to the Grammar School he's been hurting young Alec on the way home. A new lady in the valley stopped him, and Jean got really nasty outside the Briggs house. Then she began accusing me and others of denying Wilfred his chance in his year and corruptly getting George a pass."

"But that's ridiculous."

"I know. She refuses to send me a written apology for all of us, and I just don't know what I should do. I can't ignore the slander, but if I pass it up to the higher authorities, or if she does, there'll have to be an inquiry. I have nothing to hide and neither has anyone else, but it could hurt George's future happiness at the school. You heard Alice's remark about it. I just don't know what I should do."

"Let me think about this. I'll phone you on Monday morning and we'll talk further. I may be able to help. Even now, in spite of union power, a small mill owner like me is seen as God's deputy by the work force. I may be able to exert a bit of pressure if she doesn't change her mind and write the letter."

When he telephoned the school on Monday the letter hadn't been received. He discussed the situation with the headmaster, then after putting the receiver down he sent for both the Bakers.

"What's the matter, Mr. Shepherd?" Joe asked as they awaited the arrival of his wife.

"Wait until your wife arrives and you'll hear," the mill owner told him. "Sit down, Jean," he commanded a moment later as she entered the office. "I don't normally concern myself with the doings of my workers outside the mill premises, but on this occasion I must intervene. The welfare of innocent people is threatened by your doings, Jean."

"What do you mean?" she asked with anger in both her face and voice. "I've done nothing to anyone."

"You have accused several people of corruption."

"Oh that. All I've done is say a few truths that needed saying. When Wilfred was of the age to sit the exam he wasn't allowed to do so, yet that Briggs brat was urged to sit and his parents were advised to let him. He was given a pass to go to the Grammar School. His family are layabout scroungers and we'll have to pay for his education."

"Stop!" thundered her employer. "The Briggs family are decent people who've had over three years of trials since William had his accident. They are not scroungers. Your boy's a nasty cruel bully, not just to Alec but to any child smaller than himself. George Briggs wasn't given a pass, he earned it by hard work."

"No, Mr. Pighills fixed it somehow. Now he wants me to write an apology and send it to him for what I said to Gwen Briggs. I'll see him out of his job first."

"Will you? Then I've one thing to say to you. If that apology isn't properly written exonerating all those you've maligned, and on the headmaster's desk by Wednesday morning both you and Joe will be out of your jobs. I won't see a really decent family hurt by you or your son, then accused of wrong doing along with a dedicated headmaster and others, putting their careers and reputations at risk. Write and post that letter in time, or try being what you call a layabout yourself."

"Mr. Shepherd, I've not been a party to this," Joe protested. "I've worked here for you and your father before you for seventeen years. You can't sack me for what she's done."

"Yes I can. You should be the head of the house. Use the authority of a husband and a father, or be a wimp and let your wife cost you your job. If you continue to bring in a wage she'll never know what it's like to suffer as Mrs. Briggs has done. Make her write it and keep your job."

"So you're a part of it," Jean sneered. "I wondered when you took the brat in your car. Sack us, put us on the dole, and I'll still not write that letter."

"Jean, let's talk about this," Joe pleaded. "You can't mean to throw us both onto the dole queue just to satisfy your pride. Let's go home after work and think about it."

"That's sensible, Joe," his employer told him. "You're not sacked yet, so I suggest that you go back to your machines and think carefully about what you're going to do. I don't want to sack either of you, but if you don't write that letter, Jean, you're both out, and will never come back. You're including me in it now because I helped the lad when I was taking Alice to the same place. Leave me now."

CHAPTER 5

About a week later George Briggs was leaning on the timber railings of Harker's Bridge watching a dipper as it hunted for its morning feed. This was one bird whose nest he never would see, though he knew exactly where it was. Alice came to his side quietly. He had taught her to approach silently if she thought he was looking at something. She was becoming very interested in the things he showed her.

"What can you see?"

"Look there, near that old log, under the water. Do you see a bird? It'll come up for air in a moment. It's a dipper; see how it seems to curtsey all the time."

"Yes I see it. Come on now, or the train will leave us."

"We must go I suppose, but I could watch it all day. They are rather shy birds. They nest every year behind the waterfall."

As they walked up the hill he told her more about that and other birds found in or near the brook.

"How do you come to know so much about the wild creatures?"

"My father taught me a lot. When he was unemployed I often went with him gathering wood for the fire, and he showed me how to watch the birds and animals without them knowing that I was there. I also have books about the birds and other things of the British Isles. From my father and the books I learned a lot, now I go out and usually learn something as I watch."

"You've already taught me so much about the flowers and trees and the birds. I never realised how many different kinds there are around here."

"I'll lend you some of my books if you wish. I've all the books written by Romany of the B.B.C., but I've never been able to listen to his programmes because we don't have a wireless. I've several other books as well."

"Yes please, I'll take good care of them. I've never heard of Romany, but I'll ask Dad if you can come to our house and we'll listen together. Now, I've some news for you."

"What's that, Alice?"

"It's about the Bakers. When Dad called them into the office Mrs. Baker flatly refused to write the letter of apology to you all that Mr. Pighills demanded. Dad threatened to sack both of them if she didn't write it. Mr. Baker was very upset because he's worked for us a long time, both for Dad and Granddad. Dad told him to be a man and compel his wife to be reasonable.

"It seems they had a terrible row when they got home, and he told her that if he got the sack he would leave her and Wilfred and go live somewhere else. That must have frightened her because when Dad telephoned Mr. Pighills he had it. Mr. Baker is still with his wife and neither of them is sacked. If there is any more trouble about this you're to tell Mr. Pighills immediately. Dad asked me to tell you."

"That's good news. I worked hard to pass the exam and it upset me when she said those awful things. It wasn't just for me, but she could have got Mr. Pighills sacked, and we know he's a very good man. He did nothing wrong, but he did encourage me, and when Dad went to ask him about the economics if I passed he was most helpful. Your father was very kind too, and it eased my stress when he took me in the car."

"We were all pleased when he didn't have to sack them, but he said that he would have done to stop the poisonous talk. He really likes you, and was glad to be able to help you with the travelling."

The two children enjoyed their walk to the train every morning. When they got there he joined the other boys and she travelled with the girls, but they found the walk pleasant and Alice learned a lot about the wild life of the district. She was a quiet girl who, because of her father's position, had little contact with local people except at school.

George was the right kind of boy for her to travel with. His gentle nature and his love of the countryside made her feel that everything was right when she was with him. Prior to their morning walks she'd very little understanding of the creatures, trees and flowers around her. Her brother, Ernest, was eleven years older than her and assisted their father in the running of the mill.

George would have been quite happy travelling to the station alone. Unlike most boys he didn't like rough games; he much preferred to be out in the country observing nature. He agreed to walk with Alice because he felt that it was the right thing to do, and in bad weather her father's car was a great blessing. It was with great joy that he found out she was interested by the things he pointed out, and she asked sensible questions about them. After a few weeks he'd have been saddened if their daily companionship had ended. Nature watching can be a lonely occupation, and he enjoyed sharing his hobby with her.

Having to play rugby was the only thing he disliked in his school life. The games master soon realised that he hated it and would never be a talented player, but school rules said that he had to attend. Other teachers spoke highly of him and said how brilliant he was in all of his subjects, so he tried to ease the boy's problem. Of course every referee needs linesmen on the sides of the field, so he decided to try George there.

When he wasn't going to be squashed in the mud and hurt in the scrums the lad was quite content to be used in this way. He soon learned the part he had to play, and was always impartial. This was good character training for him, and it wasn't long before he was one of the officials at inter-school matches. The games master pointed out to him and the other boys that his duties were as important as any part of the game. He said that some people are suited for one thing, and others are good at something else. After that nobody objected to George being treated differently.

In almost all the other lessons he excelled. He was a quick learner and his intelligence pleased his teachers. He was very interested in learning foreign languages as well as English. He was always top of the class in French, and in his second year he found German fascinating. As Britain and France had entered the war on September 3rd, a few days before his first German lesson, there was a topical interest as well.

When Alec was old enough he easily passed the exam to join his brother at the Grammar School, but by then George was preparing for his next big test, the School Certificate examination to be taken the following summer. The two boys and Alice all walked up the hill together each morning. Mrs. Shepherd commented to Gwen when they met that it was a comfort to her knowing that the boys were with Alice on the lonely road. No woman or girl had been molested in the area in recent times, but Alice was now beginning to develop the beauty and womanly figure she would have in a few years. To know that the boys were there was pleasing to Mrs. Shepherd.

The boys also found the arrangement satisfactory. Alec wasn't as keen about wild life as his brother, but he liked it when the weather was bad and Alice's father took them to the train in the car. On these mornings he talked to the boys and encouraged them to work hard at their studies.

"You'll never again have an equal opportunity once you have left school," he told them. "You'll find that you'll need education if you're to have a successful life, and once you're working the opportunities are harder to find. Now that there's this war there'll be a shortage of teachers, so night school will be the first to be hit. Enjoy your youth, but remember that there's a future to follow. I suppose that your father has said something on these lines, but it's so important that I'm saying it too.

"You two lads are exceptional in many ways, both in your ability and your conduct. Mrs. Shepherd and I are watching your progress, and we're glad that you are accompanying Alice every day. We feel that she couldn't be safer with anyone else."

Alec was very apt with figures and had artistic abilities. This made the mill owner wonder if he might decide to enter the field of textile design when his studies ended. He said nothing to him on the subject, but he began to think how he could help him if he took that road. He knew many designers, and wondered if he'd be able to help him get a suitable position if he wanted it. That was for the future though.

George gained the Certificate without undue difficulty and after discussing the situation with his father and Mr. Shepherd he decided to continue with the foreign languages, especially the German.

By this time the war had been waged nearly a year and some of those who had left school at seventeen had been taken straight into the armed forces. At least two of those older boys whom George had known had been killed, and all young people found that there were problems in planning a future. At the other end of the age groups being called up there was a danger William might have to go, and Gwen looked on the possibility of her husband and both boys being in danger.

All the people in the valley were affected by the war, although they were far from the hostilities. London, Liverpool and other towns were bombed. When Italy came into the war a new zone of fighting began in the North African desert, and the evacuation at Dunkirk had a depressing effect on the civilian population. Wilfred had been called up with the first groups and found himself in the thick of the fighting in Egypt. One thing that affected everyone was food rationing.

"I know we're lucky to be in a place like this, so far from the bombing, but this rationing makes us remember what's happening," Gwen told Nora and Helen. "Living here we can get wild fruit and other things, and we've learned to do without whilst William was unemployed, so it will be easier for us than some, but it does remind us lads are dying, and in London and other towns people can't rest properly in air raid shelters. So far our family hasn't been made to provide men for the war, but I've three to worry about."

"Yes, things are really nasty in some towns," agreed Helen, but now Mr. Churchill's in charge I think we have a hope."

George's studies continued and he passed a scholarship for university. He hoped that he might be able to complete the course without interference by the military.

Alice had passed the School Certificate exam at the same time as George. She had no intention of continuing in higher education. Her mother wasn't in the best of health, so Alice wanted to ease her burden of running a large house and caring for four people including herself. She would also help her father with the office work of the mill; the clerk he had employed had been directed to work at a factory making aircraft components. She'd have plenty of useful work to do.

She missed the morning walks with George and Alec, and George was sorry to lose her companionship. He was at the mill house one afternoon listening to Romany's programme with Alice when her father entered the room.

"May I ask a favour of you, Mr. Shepherd?" he asked.

"Certainly, George. What is it?"

"I'd like to have your permission to visit the mill dam and the little wood beyond it."

"Yes, you may, but there are three conditions. You mustn't take any other person with you without asking me first. You must never go anywhere near the waterwheel, whether it's working or not, and you aren't allowed to fall into the dam. Alice would kill me if you drowned."

"There's another condition, Dad," Alice interjected after listening to them. "He must take me with him sometimes to show me what's there. I'm missing those walks to the train when he showed me so much."

"Now you know," her father laughed. "She's the boss around here so we must both abide by her ruling. I know she liked what you showed her, especially the chaffinch nest with the chicks in it. She read all the books that you lent her about three times each. You've made a naturalist out of my little girl."

"Yes, I showed her what was there, but it was only what we could see as we walked up the lane. There's so much more in the valley. If you allow her to come on the dam-side with me I'll be able to show her so much more. As she's a girl I didn't suggest that we should go into the big wood. You and her mother might not like the idea, and the poisonous tongues around here would soon invent some scandal. It's a pity though, because there's so much there."

"Yes, you were wise, George. Girls have to be careful, but so far as I'm concerned I've every confidence that you'd treat her as you should, and I think her mother will agree to that. As for those we won't name, I don't trust them at all, and you need to take the same care yourself. I don't just mean with Alice but in every situation. That other foolishness may be over, but some people may want revenge now or later."

After this conversation George and Alice were on the dam bank or in the little wood at least once every week when the weather was suitable. They watched the mallards and coots with their young, and especially enjoyed the tiny baby moorhen chicks. In the wood were a variety of birds, and Alice was thrilled one evening when they were lucky enough to see a mother stoat with her young.

George also taught her about the wild flowers growing near the water and at the edge of the wood, as well as the many insects that got their food from them. The trees in the wood were a mixture of oak, birch, ash and holly, with large willows and alders growing next to the stream that fed the dam. Alice was soon able to identify the various species by their leaves. When these fell off in the autumn she learned how to recognise them by their barks that all seemed to have different characteristics. After he pointed out that even as the old leaves fell off the buds for the new ones next spring were already there the winter didn't seem so dour to her.

On two occasions Mr. Shepherd came to them as they were lying in the grass watching things. He approached very quietly to avoid frightening the things they were watching, and he heard part of their whispered conversation. He pretended the meetings were coincidental, but he really wanted to check that they were only interested in the wild life. As the parent of a young girl he was taking no chances, even with a boy he liked very much. What he heard supported his trust and he felt rather mean after the second time.

George never realised why he came, but Alice did. He was surprised by George's knowledge, and his own interest was stirred when he was shown a song thrush's nest with four young birds in it. Alice was quite annoyed by his visits.

"I was surprised when you came spying on us, Dad. You told George you trusted him, then you sneak up on us to hear what he's saying to me."

"Alice, I feel somewhat ashamed myself," her father admitted, "but I feel that any father would want to do it even if he didn't. You're now a beautiful young woman. I know the law says that you're a child until you're twenty-one, but your body doesn't look like a child, and you know it has changed."

"We all have instincts and feelings, and we have to control them. Many lads don't, and they try to get the girls to follow their desires and try to please them. They don't look ahead to the possible results. I didn't think George was like that, but I had to be sure. As you were on my land I came, but I won't need to do it again."

"You certainly won't. George has only held my hand once, and that was to help me to cross the little stream that comes down from the fields above the wood. Don't spoil things, Dad. I know he's not the son of a rich man and you wouldn't want me to fall in love with him. Even so he's my friend, probably my best one. He'll be going away to university after this summer. I want him to write to me and I want to write to him.

"He'll be alone there, away from both friends and family for the very first time. He's given me so very much happiness, and I want to give him some of it back. I owe it to him to help him through the early part of his time there. He could be called into the forces, and I can't think of anything worse for a boy like him than to be in a training camp with no other person to write to beside his parents."

"That's a very good thought, Alice. Before he goes I think that your mother and I should invite him to tea one day. Ernest may be able to give him some tips about university. I can't because I was never there, I just went into the business helping Dad and it went from there. I've no objection to you two corresponding, and I don't think your mother will have.

"You said that I wouldn't want you to fall in love with him. In matters like that we don't always do what others want. If you do, and want to marry in a few years time I don't think I'll object. He's a far better person than some of the rich men's sons I know, but I advise you to keep things on the present footing for a few years. See how it turns out when he's finished his studies and you're both a little older."

"Thanks, Dad. I think I'm a little in love with him now, but I realise he's several years at the university to get through and possibility a period in the forces as well. This wretched war seems to be going on for ever. We'll have plenty of time to make the right decisions I think."

When Alice saw George a couple of days later she told him most of the conversation, but not the last part. "I was really angry when he turned up again.

It was possible that he came on us accidentally once, but not twice in such a short time. I told him so, and that it was a mean trick."

"Be fair, Alice. He's your father, and he probably saw it as his duty to check me out. I don't blame him. On the dam side we're in the open and anyone can see us, but in the wood we could be doing anything. You're a very lovely young woman now, and he feels a real need to protect you. I feel very lucky he allows us to come out like this."

"Well I thought he insulted you, but it's turned out for the best. We had a talk about things and he doesn't object to me writing to you when you go away. In fact, he thinks that it would be good for you to come to tea one day before you leave. He says Ernest may be able to give you some tips to help you to settle in."

"There, you see he's not so bad after all. He helped me before, and he wants to do it again. But he doesn't want me to steal his daughter, and who can blame him for that? Now, forget all that, there's a kingfisher on that hazel bush."

A few days after they had seen the kingfisher George and Alice were in a new hide that he had built close to the dam and fairly near the mill. They'd been there for a quarter of an hour when George spotted something special.

"Look, Alice, there's a heron next to the hawthorn. We'll watch it for a while to see if it catches anything."

Alice looked where George had indicated and saw the tall grey bird walking sedately over the grassy bank of the stream.

"It reminds me of an old man, one with a slight stoop as he walks," she said. "What's it doing? In pictures we always see them standing by the water looking for fish."

"It's hunting for frogs or anything small enough to swallow. Frogs are a favourite food for herons."

As they watched the bird calmly walked about, occasionally it stopped to look around for danger. After a while it found a frog and ate it before flying away with a slow beat of its huge wings.

"That was really interesting," Alice said. "I've never seen one before, but all your books showed them."

"They aren't rare, but they're rather shy. If it heard us it would have left sooner."

"When do you go to university?"

"Early September. I'm looking forward to it, but at the same time I'm apprehensive. There'll be so much that's new. I've always slept at home and been with my family. As you know I usually get on well with young people, but I like to spend some time alone. I understand that there are marshes fairly close, so I'll see birds new to me, and that's good. I certainly won't be joining the major sporting groups unless it's mandatory. In all but really bad weather I get my exercise walking."

"That's why Mum and Dad want you to come to tea one day before you go. Ernest was at Cambridge, but not in the same part as you'll be. He may be able to tell you some things that will ease your anxiety and help you to settle in. When we finish here today you must come into the house to arrange it."

For another half hour they stayed in the hide watching various birds and a water vole that was swimming close to the bank. When they left George went into the mill house and was greeted by both of Alice's parents.

"Did you see anything special today," her father asked.

"Yes, I saw my first heron. It wasn't fishing, but we watched it swallow a frog. George says that they often eat them. We also watched a water vole for a while."

"He's making a really keen naturalist of you."

"Yes, I'll miss him when he goes away. I don't think I'll want to go to those isolated places too much by myself."

"You need to be careful. Even on our own land you could have a nasty situation if some of the lads knew you were alone. Most are decent, but not all of them."

"I'd be very upset if my teaching you about wild life led to you being hurt in any way," George told her.

"Don't worry about that," Mrs. Shepherd told him. "You've given her a great deal of pleasure and helped her to understand the things around her. A young woman can be at risk anywhere if she allows situations to arise. If she stays away from lonely places she should be in no more danger than any other girl. If she takes risks and suffers for it you'll not be to blame."

"I brought George home so that you can arrange that meal you mentioned," Alice told her father. "It'll not be long now before he has to leave."

"Yes, George," Mr Shepherd said, "Ernest feels that he may be able to ease your anxieties and smooth your entry into university life as he's been there. We thought it would be nice if you came to tea one day soon. Perhaps your parents would like to come as well, in fact all of you would be welcome."

"I'd certainly like to come, but I can't speak for the others. If Dad comes it'll have to be on a day when he's off duty at the pub. Shall I ask them and tell you next time I see one of you?"

"If you please, George."

When George told his family they were surprised.

"We must accept. This is very considerate of Ernest and all of them," William said. "I'll check with Nigel which days I'll be free."

"I don't see a lot of benefit in my spending an evening there," Alec said. "Perhaps it would be better if you three went without me."

"Don't be too hasty, lad," William warned. "Mr. Shepherd is taking a lot of interest in George, and has done for some time. He's a business man, truly a small one, but he knows people. You'll want the best employment you can get, and any advice that he decides to give you should be listened to very carefully. This is the time of your life when decisions made can affect all of your future for good or ill. I know the war is making it almost impossible to plan ahead at your age, but it'll not last for ever. Please yourself, but in your shoes I'd go."

"I hadn't looked at it like that, Dad. Yes, I'll go. Even if I gain nothing they'll be pleased if we all go; that may help George some way either now or later."

"That's good thinking," Gwen said. "We don't know what could come of this for any of us, and especially George. It's good you're thinking of him as well as yourself; that's how a good family should be."

William's next day off was on a Sunday. George told the Shepherds and it was convenient for them. Dressed in their best clothes all the family walked the short distance to the mill house. After their humble dwelling with its primitive assets and well worn furnishings the home of the mill owner seemed like a palace. They were welcomed by both Mr. and Mrs. Shepherd and George got a special greeting from their daughter.

"Thank you, Mrs. Shepherd, for inviting us all, and for your continuing concern for George's success," Gwen said.

"My name is Edith to my friends, and you probably know that my husband is Walter. We want this to be an informal meeting, and know you'll use discretion when amongst the people of the valley."

"Thank you. I'm Gwen and my husband is William. Of course you know George and his brother is Alec."

Whilst they were getting to know each other better Alice was laying the table for the meal. Nobody except George and Alice knew how it began, but they all noticed that the girl had obtained the help of her friend in setting out the various items of equipment and food.

"Hello," Walter said, "our Alice is getting George trained for some woman to use. Watch it, lad, or she'll work you to death."

"There could be worse fates," the victim of his humour replied.

"I'm not training him for some woman, Dad. When he's been through university and got a very high salaried job I may want him myself. Just in case I'm making sure that he knows how to be a slave."

"Let's hope that he does get a job like that," Ernest put in. "I went to that same university in another part, and all I ended up with is being a very underpaid slave of Walter Shepherd."

As the company laughed at this remark Alice called them to the table. This sobered the conversation and all enjoyed the meal. The food was plain and nourishing and the Briggs family were pleased that nothing exotic had been put on the menu. They were happy to be treated as equals by all the Shepherds. When the meal was finished and there was a break in the conversation Walter turned to George.

"Now, lad, are you ready to leave all this and go have a few words with our Ernest before that slaver finds you some washing up to do?"

"Yes, I'm ready if he is."

The two young men left the table and Ernest led the way into a smaller room.

"This is my den," he told George. "No woman is allowed to come in here and disturb my things. I even dust the shelves and clean the windows myself. "

"Then I'm honoured to be brought in here."

"We need to be able to talk without distractions. Before we start on the university will you answer one personal question for me?"

"If I can."

"I've known for a while that you and Alice have been friendly and you've taught her a lot about the wild life of this area. After what she said about training you I wonder what the situation is. My sister is very dear to me. I know that was said in a joking context, but is there some truth in her words?"

"To a degree it's serious. We like each other, but I realise that she's the daughter of an industrialist and even now that Dad's working he only earns a barman's wages. I'm very fond of her, and I think that the feeling is mutual, but it'll be years, if ever, before I get an income worthy of her. Until and unless I do get that income all thoughts of anything but friendship is foolish, but should I get success and she happens to still be free I'll certainly try to build our friendship into a marriage.

"Of course there's also the possibility that I'll be called up. I may have to go and spend years in the forces, perhaps be killed or crippled for life. I can't make any plans with her that could cause her to be married to a helpless cripple or become a widow, nor have I the right to claim her fidelity to a man who'll be in the forces for many years. On the other hand we now have some support from the Americans, thanks to the Japs. Pearl Harbour may bring peace so much sooner."

"That's a fair answer. I'll let you into a secret, she's very much attracted to you. Only last week she turned down a friend of mine when he asked her to go out with him. She told him as kindly as she could that there's only one man who interests her. Although she didn't name you I know that you're the one she was thinking of. She told me that she'll be writing to you whilst you're away. Please don't ever hurt her."

"I've no intention of doing that I can assure you, but there'll be years of hard work and study before I can think of settling down with a wife. In that time she could meet up with someone else, so I mustn't think too seriously about our future yet, or I could be the one who's hurt, and it wouldn't be her fault."

"Now we've got that off our chests, and I for one will never disclose what you've said unless I see a need for it in the future. Let us talk about university life now. I wasn't in the same part of the complex as you will be, but there are several factors common to all. You can get accommodation on the campus, or try to obtain lodgings off it. The trouble with on campus is you've no control over your close neighbours with whom you've to share certain facilities. I'd no trouble, but I did see one or two unpleasant incidents with others. It'll depend on what you can afford. Try not to get into debt; it takes a lot of getting rid of. Are you interested in sport?"

"Not very much. I hated rugby until the sports master made me a permanent linesman. I had to be on the field, but it was alright when I didn't have to be involved with the actual game."

"There are plenty of other activities and I'd advise you to find something that interests you. You can't study all of your free time, you'd become stale. There are chess and draughts clubs, amateur theatricals and many others."

"Yes, and there are fens not too far away with many birds that I've never seen. I'll almost certainly get most of my exercise there, both physical and mental, when the weather allows."

"If that's what you want there's a society for that as well. I'd advise you to join it for at least the first year, for your own safety. Some parts are dangerous and you need to understand the fens before you go out alone.

"There's also a students' bar. I don't drink, except toasts at weddings, but if you like a beer it's run on a non-profit system. Of course you can go and have a soft drink if you want the company. Be very careful and always remember why you're there. Some go to university to learn, gain accreditation for a good job, but they forget and begin to think they can neglect lectures and personal study to have what they see as a good time.

"You're from Harker's Bridge and have known poverty, it would be too easy to go the wrong way and throw away your opportunity. I don't want to sound like an old spoilsport, but I saw people who set out with the zeal you seem to have. They made the wrong sort of friends and got nowhere. One lad I knew and really liked got into the wrong set and had trouble with a female from another college and had to go home.

"I think that your correspondence with Alice will help you. Let your hopes for the future with her drive you to stay on course. Be careful, there are many traps, but enjoy yourself. There are opportunities to make those years fruitful and a happy part of your life you'll remember for many years. End of lecture. Any questions?"

"No, I think you have covered all of mine, and a few others beside. Thank you, and thank you for what you said about my friendship with your sister."

"In that case we'll rejoin the others. Do you know that yours is the only family in Harker's Bridge that has ever come here as guests? Dad has really come to like you all."

"The feeling is mutual. He made my life a lot easier on the day of the County Minor exam. I was dreading having to go to find the place more than the test itself, and he removed all of that when he took me in your car. I might not have passed without that. Since then he's been kindness itself and allowed Alice and me to enjoy this valley together. He's been a real friend."

+ + +

Alec obtained his School Certificate and stayed on for further studies. William had to register, and was called to have a medical examination. His eyesight got him exemption from call-up, which was a relief for all the family. Overall the Briggs family were in a better position than many.

Alec's studies at the Grammar School were also completed before military duties were imposed on him. By then the nations were at peace and he found them a means of seeing part of Europe. William and Gwen were pleased because both their sons had obtained certificates that could help them to a better life than their parents had endured for several years.

CHAPTER 6

The time came when the extension to the pub was coming to completion and Frank Dobson moved some men to other sites. When William had fixed the last tap and Frank had no more work for him the plumber became a full-time member of the bar staff. Nigel Holdsworth was now his only employer. As the new section wouldn't be opened immediately he continued to work with Percy. Sometimes he was asked to do other tasks as they were needed.

The last part of the work of the builders was an increase in the size of the car park. It was very small, and Nigel decided that although it was rarely used there could be a need for a larger one when the hall was in use. As people with higher incomes attended the business meetings taking place there he expected to see more cars, and there was always the possibility that more of the less well off would become car owners. He didn't want them to take their business elsewhere because there was nowhere to park the vehicles. Once this task was completed the last of the builder's men left the area and only the regulars and casual visitors appeared in the bar.

William found his new employment reasonably interesting. He learned how to care for the beer, tap barrels and change them when they were empty, and also how to clean the pipes to the pumps. He also had to learn the art of dealing with all types of customers. As most of them at this time were regulars, and at first his own recent work-mates, there were few problems, but as Percy pointed out most of his clients in the new bar would be from outside the area and from all stations of life.

Percy was a good teacher, and the two men soon became friends. Nigel tried to spend a short time each afternoon with his bar staff, and part of the evenings meeting his customers. He was pleased with his new employee, and one day when it was William's day off he discussed the man with Percy.

"How do you think he'll settle in his own bar?" he asked.

"He should be alright with Elsie. I don't think it would be wise to put him on alone at first. He sometimes works alone on here, but only whilst I have my lunch, and this is mostly beer sales. He's getting to know the regulars, but when he goes on the new one there'll be many strangers and some of them will want unfamiliar drinks. Some will be pleasant, but others could be arrogant snobs. He hasn't met that sort yet.

"If Elsie isn't available he should have another experienced person with him at first, even if trade is slow. Give him time to build up confidence, then if someone asks for a drink that he doesn't know he'll be able to handle the situation. I had one in here only last week. He wanted a drink that I'd never heard of before. I told him if he had the recipe I would make it, but as he didn't he settled for a gin and tonic."

"Yes, I think you're right. We don't want to spoil a good and honest man, and Frank Dobson says he's both. Has he met Elsie yet?"

"They were together on this bar last week on my day off. Neither of them appeared to be wounded when I saw them later. Elsie's a very nice person, and I think William is the same."

"Well if the scars don't show that's good enough for me," Nigel laughed as he left the room.

When the last of the builders left the site Nigel gave temporary employment to some local people who were to give the new building a thorough cleaning from top to bottom. The new bar was stocked with bottled beer, soft drinks, spirits and other things. Sherries and wines were also made available. The two beer pumps were connected to the barrels, and all was made ready for the opening night. Seating had been purchased for the hall, and a few tables and chairs were placed outside it for those wanting a drink. Opening night was a Friday, and a local councillor had agreed to perform the ceremony.

"His fee and the drinks he and his wife are supplied will be well covered by the publicity he'll get for us," Nigel told his staff. "Some of his cronies will probably come with him, and there are no better drinkers of shorts than politicians. That's the main reason why they like election nights. It gives them the perfect reason to either celebrate or commiserate over a double scotch."

There was to be a dance after the opening, and the promoter would take the door money to pay for the band and his own expenses and profit. If he did well he was ready to book the hall on a regular basis for weekly dances.

William wore a white jacket and a black bow tie, and Elsie had a white blouse above a black skirt as they awaited their first customer.

"Are you nervous? It's a big occasion," Elsie enquired.

"A little. I'm getting to know the people in the other bar, but these will be mostly strangers. Some of them will be what are called the upper class and may be difficult to please."

"They're no better than us, and you must remember that you're the one in charge. Don't be arrogant about it, but if one of them gets obnoxious you must be firm. The majority will be nice people, but if you do get into difficulty I'm here to rescue and support you. Try to relax and enjoy."

They had a steady trickle of customers before the opening ceremony, then there was a lull whilst the speeches were made. William found that he could handle the work very well. The only differences between this bar and the other were that the customers were better dressed and more of them were drinking spirits, sherries and fruit juices. After the opening a few non-dancers came out for a beer or other refreshment. From then on there was a steady stream of customers.

About eight o'clock Constance Manning came out of the hall. She was wearing a flowered dress and her blonde hair was set in a girlish style that didn't really suit her age. Her companion was a tall dark man wearing a light blue suit and a flashy tie. Elsie served them.

"What would you like to drink?" the man asked her.

"Oh, I think I would like a gin and tonic with ice and lemon please," she replied in a kind of speech she wouldn't have used when gossiping with Jean Baker.

They emptied their glasses and returned to the dance floor. On three further occasions she returned; each time she had a different man paying for the drink. The last time Elsie was temporarily away from the bar and William attended to their requirements.

"I didn't know that you were a barman," she told him. "I thought that you were a plumber."

"I was, but when that work ended I was offered this job. It's better than being unemployed, even though your neighbour thinks that we're scroungers and like to live off the state."

"What time will you finish work?" she asked. "Jim has to leave after we finish the drink, so we can walk home together. I'm not very keen on walking down that dark lane alone."

"I'm afraid we can't do that, Constance. For one thing I want no rumours spreading around. There's always at least one poisonous gossip, as we have recently experienced. You go home at the end of the dance. It'll be much later when I leave. We've to tidy up the place ready for the cleaner in the morning, and also see to the beer pumps. Then we all go into the other room and the boss gives a drink to all who want one. The main thing is we can chat together and unwind after a long evening's work. It could be after midnight when I leave."

As they conversed Elsie returned and heard the end of William's words.

"What was all that about?"

"I think she was trying to set me up for a scandal. She wanted to walk home with me 'down that dark lane' as she put it. I'm sure she was a party to the false accusations we had to deal with about George's scholarship. I'm not falling for it."

"You're right. Be careful, she's poison. I'll tell you more when we've time."

Nigel was very pleased with the success of the evening. All had gone well and there'd been no trouble makers. The main debris had been cleared away and after all the glasses had been washed the staff joined their employer in Percy's bar.

"We've had a very good opening night both for ourselves and the dance promoter," Nigel told them. "You were fine, William. I saw you serving various mixed drinks and you seemed confident. You'll be a very good barman before long."

"Yes," Elsie agreed. "He's coming along well. I only had to help him once when a lady wanted a snowball. He made a second one for her later, but I was there watching. We get along fine together."

"That's good to hear," Nigel told her.

"Now, William, I want to tell you about that matter we spoke about earlier, so if you others will excuse us we'll leave you all for a little while. We'll not be long," Elsie said.

They moved to a table at the other end of the room, "Now let me show you how poisonous she is. She's a gold digger. Tonight she had four different men spending money on her, and I think that she left the hall with some of them. Before she came to Harker's Bridge she lived close to my cousin, and she tried to lead him astray because he's fairly well off financially. When he wouldn't bite she started a rumour about him and another woman that really upset his wife. Fortunately I was able to prove that she was lying, but it was all very nasty.

"She knows it was me who sorted it all out, so we must both be on our guard. She may try to link our names since we've both spoiled her plans. I stopped her hurting my family, and you rejected her. We must treat her like any other customer, but also be on the watch for treachery all the time. Watch for her poisonous tricks, I'm sure they'll come."

"I believe you're right. One thing I'll do is tell Gwen about her ploy tonight and what you have told me, then she'll be prepared for her tricks. We have a wonderful marriage and two good lads. Nobody will spoil that or hurt any of us if I can avoid it."

+++

It was Monday morning and Gwen Briggs had sent Alec to school with Nora. She transferred all the hot water from the large container on the gas ring to the peggy-tub and re-filled the huge pan before placing it back on the gas. She then put soap flakes into the tub and dropped in a batch of white and light coloured clothes. As she was doing so Helen Field came into the room. She took hold of the posser, a large plunger fastened to the end of a stout broomstick.

Good morning, Gwen. I seem to have just timed it right to help you."

She put the posser into the tub and forced the water to run through the clothes a few times. "Now," she said, "feed the garments into the wringer and I'll turn the handle. That way you'll be done in half the time."

"Never stop a good volunteer," Gwen said. "I seem to have more to wash now. William has to have clean white shirts and since he went to his new school George is more conscious of his clothes. Mum gets busier, but we're all well and happy. Fortunately Nigel sends the smocks William wears on the bar to the laundry.

"George is quite rightly preparing himself for the kind of life he hopes to lead. He wants to obtain some kind of job involving foreign languages, perhaps as a translator or something of that nature. If not he could become a teacher at a school like the one he attends. Either way he'll need to be conscious of his clothes and hair style. Even now he's mixing with boys from upper class homes and is sometimes invited to visit them.

"He's much happier now that he's a permanent linesman in the rugby lessons. He's learning a job that's apparently important to both teams, and it's teaching him how to make responsible decisions affecting other people. He sees it as a service to the other boys, and much more to his taste than being in the game. William is happy because he isn't unemployed again. He likes meeting people and gets on well with both Percy on the old bar and the woman he's working with on the new."

"Is he at work now?"

"No, today is his day off. He's gone to the garden to fetch some vegetables. Here he comes now."

William took good care to thoroughly clean his boots before entering the cottage. He placed a large basket in one corner of the room well away from the laundry team.

"I've brought the first of the broad beans," he told Gwen, "and there's a lettuce for you, Helen. You may as well have one of the spares before they're spoiled by going up to seed."

"Thank you. Gwen says this is your day off. What will you do with it?"

"I was going to do what you are doing, but now I'll go to get some wood for the fire. There should be plenty of windfalls after that gale the other night. First though I'll have a cup of tea."

"Put the kettle on the fire," Gwen told him. "I need the gas to keep my hot water supply going."

"Do you like being behind the bar?" Helen enquired.

"It's interesting when I'm on the new one which is mine and Elsie's. When that's closed we both take turns on the old one, but on our own we meet all kinds of people, especially when it's a meeting or a wedding reception. Elsie's a good workmate, and as I'm still a novice she's teaching me and looking after me. I never realised how many different mixed drinks there are, and some of them have the strangest names."

"How are the Friday dances going? I thought of coming up sometime."

"They're becoming popular. Your friend Constance is a regular supporter."

"Does she dance, or is she just chasing men?"

"Now don't be spiteful, Helen. She dances, but usually with those she thinks have a fat wallet and will be willing to open it. I think that she likes to lead them to the bar."

"I like a dance, so perhaps I'll come up this week."

"This Friday is all old time dances, next week is 50/50 and the third week is all modern ballroom. Nigel says the promoter considers it best to do it this way at first, until he knows what the customers prefer."

By now the tub was empty so William poured out the water and re-filled it for the rinsing. Once these clothes were through more soap flakes would be added for the coloured clothes to be washed. This saved a heating of water, and once they were finished a final supply of clean water would rinse them and then be used to swill the stone flags outside the cottage. Nothing was wasted, and as much work as possible was done for the effort and gas used. Whilst he was helping with the heavier lifting Helen made his tea which he drank as soon as it was cool enough.

"Now I'll go see what I can find in the woods," he said. "As Helen is here I may stay a while to get some fresh air and enjoy the wild life. George found a couple of new nests last week, so I'll try to locate them."

When he returned with a large branch on his shoulder the washing was finished and the clothes were dancing merrily on the clothes line from the house to an iron pole close to the boundary wall of the field. After they were dried sufficiently Gwen would heat the flat irons on the fire and use them to press those items that needed it. Mondays weren't easy for the women of the valley.

+ + +

The following Friday Helen decided to attend the dance as it was a fine evening for walking up the lanes. She was a good dancer of both the old time and the ballroom dances, but she preferred the stately kind like the valeta and the maxina.

"Hello, Helen," she heard a voice behind her as she stood near the door looking round the room. She turned and saw a tall young woman with reddish hair and wearing a flowered dress.

"Molly, what a nice surprise. I haven't seen you for ages. How are you?"

"I'm fine. These weekly dances are a real treat, just what the area needed. Do you come often?"

"This is my first time."

"It's mine too, but I don't think it'll be the last."

"Come for a drink. It's nice when there's a place where we women can enjoy a glass of something without being considered common, as we would be in most pubs if we'd no man with us. As it happens the barman is a very good friend of mine. We're next door neighbours and they're a really nice family."

They both enjoyed the evening. The band was a good one, and as they were both competent dancers they'd plenty of partners. They agreed to meet the next week and Friday evenings became a highlight for them. In September Helen went for a holiday in the Highlands of Scotland north of Inverness. The weather was mixed, but that didn't matter as she was visiting her only sister and her family.

"I wish you could stay longer," Margaret said when Helen decided that she needed to return home after three weeks.

"No doubt that you do, sister, but if I don't go now it'll start snowing and I'll be stuck here all winter."

"That would be fine, but I suppose I must let you go to that lonely life you lead down in Yorkshire. If you stayed all winter we would find you a nice strong Scot who would keep you from being lonely. When will you get married, Helen? Being single is alright, but marriage with the right man is better."

"Maybe it is, but I haven't met Mr. Right yet. I'm not so lonely now. I've new neighbours who have two lovely boys, and the whole family are very nice people."

The trains ran well and were on time, but it's a long way from northern Scotland to Yorkshire. She enjoyed the scenery when the rhythm of the wheels and the sound of the steam engines didn't lull her to sleep. She was tired when she stepped off the train at Leeds City Station and that may have been the reason why she didn't place her foot onto the platform properly. It seemed to turn over as it took her weight. She nearly fell, but an alert porter noticed and caught her.

The ankle was badly sprained, so one of the first aid crew bandaged it firmly. She was then taken to Central Station where she was to catch her local train. A message was sent to her final station for someone to help her when she arrived. Not only was there a porter waiting with a wheelchair but a taxi had been summoned to take her right home. Though it wasn't their fault the accident had occurred the driver had been told to send a bill for the fare to the railway company.

With the exception of Mr. Shepherd's car that never went near the cottages it was a rare occasion when any car was seen by the residents of Harker's Bridge. When the taxi drew up Gwen heard it and looked through the window. She saw the driver go around the vehicle to help Helen so she went out immediately.

"Are you alright, Helen?"

"No, I sprained my ankle badly in Leeds."

The driver had opened the cottage door and he and Gwen helped Helen inside and sat her on the sofa. After bringing in her case the driver left.

"Now let me have a look at that foot," Gwen ordered.

When the stocking had been removed they saw that there was a lot of swelling. The shoe had been left off because once the bandage was put on in Leeds it was too small. The whole foot was an awful colour.

"I think you should have a doctor for this," Gwen told her. It's obviously a bad injury, and a small bone may be damaged. We'll leave the bandage on as it was put there by a trained person, but even with it on we can see that this is serious."

"I think that if there had been a broken bone the first aid man would have said something, but perhaps I should have a doctor to see it. Will you go to the mill and ask Mr. Shepherd to telephone Dr. Grant please?"

Mr. Shepherd wasn't surprised by the request as his was the only telephone in the valley.

"Dr. Grant is on his way," he told Gwen. "There's no need to pay for the call; we should all help when someone's hurt."

Gwen hurried home to be there when the doctor arrived and soon his car was seen coming down the lane.

"I don't think anything is broken," the doctor told Helen after examining the foot, "but there are many small bones in this part of the foot. If I sent you for an Xray they could do nothing until the swelling goes down and the bruise clears. I'll strap it up again and see what happens in the next few days. I'll come again in three days. Until then you must stay in bed except for getting food and toilet needs. We'll get you up the stairs now."

"She doesn't need to get out of bed at all," Gwen told him. "I live next door and we've a bedpan she can use." When he came again Dr. Grant was pleased to see that the swelling was going down, and much of the bruise had cleared.

"That's much better," he told her after he had again felt the bones of the damaged area. "You can get up now and with help go downstairs if you will quietly sit on the sofa when you get there. You mustn't try to go either up or down the stairs alone. I'll see you in about a week."

Helen would have found life very tedious if the Briggs family and Nora hadn't given her all their spare time. She also had her wireless and plenty of books.

"If it didn't give me so much pain I'd do this regularly," Helen told Nora one morning. "I feel like a queen with all you people looking after me."

"Feel that way if you must," Nora told her, but don't think that we'll all wear a uniform and curtsy to you. I'm an Irish woman from Dublin, and we Irish don't want English kings and queens, and that would include you."

"In that case I must stay as I am," laughed Helen. "If I can't get proper service and respect I suppose there's nothing else to do but get better."

When Dr. Grant came again he examined the ankle and declared himself satisfied that nothing was broken. "Does that hurt?" he asked.

"A little, but not like it did."

"Good. Keep it bandaged for two or three weeks and don't try to walk on it too much at first. You can hobble on it with a stick for short distances like ten or twenty yards, but no serious walking yet. If it starts to be painful cut out the activity until it stops. It'll tell you if you do too much. Unless you send for me I'll not come again."

Fortunately she didn't need to send for him, and slowly the pain went away. Gwen and Nora made sure that she'd all she needed without having to walk further than to the outdoor toilet or into the Briggs home. She began to go there and help Gwen with jobs that could be done sitting down like darning socks or cutting up old clothes for rug making. Later she was able to stand to do the washing up or ironing the white shirts of William and George.

"You don't need to slave away like that," Gwen told her in the hearing of Nora. You're still an invalid."

"Let her slave," Nora said. She'd come around the block to visit her friends a while before going to collect the children. "She'd have all of us slaving, and if I hadn't put my foot down she'd have had us all in uniform and curtseying. She said that she felt like a queen and that's what they always want."

"Nora, you're awful. Trust a woman from Dublin to torture a poor cripple."

The three ladies enjoyed the short spell of humour and leg-pulling. Helen had an easy life normally, but the other two had to work really hard to care for their families and keep their homes clean with primitive equipment and medieval water heating systems. They needed to be able to laugh occasionally.

CHAPTER 7

Four weeks after Dr. Grant's final visit Helen made a decision.

"William, is there a dance at the pub tonight?"

"Yes, it's old time only."

"I think I'll come up. I've walked quite a bit these last few days without any problem. I'll patronise the bar and have a rest, then see how it feels to dance, if I get a partner."

"Be careful," Gwen warned her anxiously. "Don't try too much too soon."

"I won't. If there's the least twinge I'll stop."

"See that you do. Can you keep an eye on her, William?"

"Only when she's in the lounge, we aren't in the hall. I'll ask Nigel to watch her."

Half an hour after the hall doors opened Helen arrived and went straight through to the bar. She bought a drink and sat at one of the tables.

"How does your foot feel after walking up the lanes?" William asked.

"There hasn't been even a hint of trouble. I'll sit here for a while before I try dancing."

"Just the man I want to see," William said as Nigel walked into the room.

"Is something wrong?"

"Not yet, but Miss Field has had a sprained ankle. She's our next door neighbour. She thinks that she's now fit enough to try a few dances, so if you are in the hall will you make sure that she isn't overdoing it? I don't want to carry her home."

"I'll watch when I'm there." He turned to Helen, "If you find that you are in difficulty I'll order a taxi to save poor William's back. If I'm not there tell Elsie or William and they'll contact me."

"Thank you. I hope I'll not be such a nuisance. I won't dance very much tonight, but life has been so very boring these last six weeks. I can watch the others when I rest."

She handed her empty glass to Elsie and went into the hall. Molly saw her enter and immediately came to her. "How lovely it is to see you here again. I thought you went to Scotland for just two weeks. Where have you been all this time?"

"Margaret made me stay three weeks, then I sprained my ankle getting off the train at Leeds. I've been housebound for weeks and got really fed up. I'll not be dancing much tonight, but I need the company."

"Now's your chance to test it; the next dance is the Moonlight Saunter. That's about as slow as they come. Shall we go in together?"

"That's a good idea. If I need to stop it'll be better with you than one of the men."

The band began to play and the young women were amongst the first on the floor. Helen felt no pain and really enjoyed dancing again. As they were sitting out of the following Gay Gordons they looked around the hall. Constance was there, and was talking with a tall handsome young man wearing a medium blue lounge suit.

"Your friend is here," Molly remarked.

"She's no friend of mine. Who's the good looking fellow she's with? I've never seen him before."

"No, you won't have, because he's only been here three weeks. He's an author, and is staying in the rooms upstairs."

"He's very handsome and looks really smart in that suit."

Just then two young men came to ask them to dance in the valeta, and this was Helen's favourite dance. After it they had other partners, but if the dance offered was a robust one Helen would ask the man to come for an easier one. She enjoyed the evening, but later began to feel sharp pains in the ankle.

"That's enough," she told Molly. "I felt a sharp pain in that one as I turned."

There were only two more dances before the interval, so they both went to the bar before the rush.

"Are you alright?" William asked anxiously.

"Yes, but I'll not dance any more tonight. The foot is tiring, and I still have to walk home."

"That'll be best. Remember what the boss said, don't overdo it."

Whilst they sat at a table they watched Constance come to the bar with a man. She had left the author and her new companion bought her a gin and tonic.

"She hasn't lost her touch," Helen told Molly.

"Far from it, she's an expert at getting men to spend money on her."

They ate some food before returning to the hall where Molly found plenty of partners and Helen watched and chatted with various friends. Constance had returned to the author. He'd taken her onto the floor once and she seemed as if she wanted to repeat the experience, but he didn't seem interested. He was talking with other people and she was hovering nearby. Suddenly he left the group with whom he'd spent most of the evening and Helen realised that he was heading in her direction. Molly was dancing, so it was clear that she was his target.

"Good evening," he said in a pleasant voice. "I wonder if you would like to dance. You haven't been on the floor since before the interval, and when you were up I noticed that you're an accomplished dancer."

"Thank you, but I'll not be doing any more this evening. If you wish to speak with me a little while please sit down, but I've had a badly sprained ankle. It's telling me that we've done enough for the first time. I still have to walk home."

"I understand that your name is Miss Field," he said as he took the chair next to hers. "Mine is Richard Moulding, and I'm staying in this pub for a while in the new rooms above the hall. I'm an author, and I'm doing research for a novel, part of it will be based on this district. I'm also working on another that my publisher will want quite soon. I'm a bit late with it as I've been ill."

"My friends call me Helen," she told him. "I saw you talking with Miss Manning. She's a neighbour of mine, but she doesn't seem to like me for some reason. William on the bar lives next door to me, and he and his family are good friends of mine. They and an Irish lady who hasn't been in the valley long have looked after me when I couldn't walk at all."

"Is your foot hurting now?"

"Not as it has been, but in that last waltz I felt a couple of warning twinges that told me I've done enough for today. I've strict orders from William, his wife and Mr. Holdsworth not to overdo it, so I must obey."

"Quite right too. I've some liniment in my room I was given when I had a similar accident recently. It's no use to me now, but its wonderful stuff, so I'll fetch it for you."

"Thank you, you're very kind."

He arose and left her, returning a few minutes later with a small jar. As he passed near Constance she tried to waylay him, but he kept on walking. She watched as he walked back to Helen, then she turned away with a disgusted look on her face. He gave the jar to Helen who placed it in her handbag and again thanked him.

"As you're not dancing may I buy you a drink? We can talk for a short while and get to know each other."

"Thank you, that will be nice, but if I know Constance it'll not be long before she tries to reclaim you."

"She can't because I was never hers to reclaim. I give her the odd dance out of courtesy, but she's always trying to monopolise me. Sometimes she's in the bar if I visit it at lunchtime, and she seems to be a bit friendly with Mrs. Holdsworth. When she's there I've difficulty in getting rid of her without being rude."

Helen told Molly where she was going, then she left the hall with Richard. He knew William as the barman, but Helen introduced them formally.

"I've been hearing very nice things about you and your family," Richard told William.

"If she's been talking about us helping her these last few weeks it was only what any decent neighbour would do. I'm willing to bet she didn't tell you how she's helped Gwen every week since we moved into the valley. Only last Monday I saw her turning the handle on the mangle." He turned to Helen, "If you wait until we close the bar I'll leave early and walk down the lane with you. It'll be about half an hour after the bar shuts."

"You told me that you refused to walk down with Constance."

"This is different, and you're not Constance. If your foot got worse when you were half way home there'd be nobody else around to help you."

"It'll give Constance and Jean food for gossip."

"That doesn't worry me. We'll know what they say is false, and Gwen will know it. Nobody else matters."

"I've an even better idea," interjected the author. "If you think you can trust me I can take you to your home in my car."

"There's no need for you to go to that trouble," Helen protested. "I'll be alright, especially with William to help if I need it."

"Why flog an already weary ankle when there's a car doing nothing? Please let me help you, if you think I can be trusted with a beautiful young woman at night. It won't take enough petrol to matter, and I haven't yet started on this month's ration."

"Of course I trust you. Alright I accept, but if William is to go with us we'll have to wait a while for him."

"No, Helen, I'll stay and have my usual half hour with the staff. You go home, and take that foot to bed where it can rest."

Richard stayed with Helen when they returned to the hall. When she was not dancing Molly joined them, and Richard partnered her in a set of Lancers that formed close to where they were sitting, so Helen was able to watch them. Others came to talk to her, and after her long stay in the house she found it all very enjoyable.

She went to the 'Ladies', and on her return she felt pain in the ankle. Molly noticed a slight limp as she approached her seat. "Is it hurting now?" she asked.

"A little, but not too bad. I'm pleased that I don't have to walk home on it."

"Look," Richard said, "it's now 9.30. The dance goes on until 11, but it may be wiser to go home now and go to bed."

"But that would deprive you of the last hour."

"I'm not worried about that. If I wish I can return in a very short time."

"Perhaps you should go," Molly agreed. "It may be better to cut it short and be able to come next week."

Richard went to fetch his car from the garage. He brought it round to the door of the hall. Molly went to tell William her friend had decided to go home whilst Richard took Helen to the car. As he came to fetch her Constance tried again to snare him, but he ignored her. He just kept on walking; when she saw him leaving with Helen she looked really angry. If looks could kill Helen would have died very quickly. By the time that she'd walked across the hall and negotiated the three steps down from the hall door the limp had increased. A few minutes later the car moved away as Helen waved to an anxious Molly.

+ + +

When they arrived at Harker's Bridge Richard stopped the car outside Helen's door.

"Give me your key and I'll unlock the door whilst you get out of the car," he ordered.

As she put her foot to the ground he heard her gasp.

"Is it worse?"

"It seems so. I shouldn't have gone so soon. I think it was those three steps outside the hall that did it."

"Then let me help you," he said as he placed an arm around her waist. "Lean on me and let me take your weight." When they were inside he led her to the sofa. "It's a good job that you didn't try to walk home on it. These things soon object if you tire them too much. Now, whilst I turn my back you remove your shoe and stocking, then I'll put some of that liniment on it."

Carefully and gently the man put on the unguent before bandaging the ankle.

"Are you having any supper?"

"No, I'd enough at the interval."

"In that case I'll carry you up to the bedroom, you don't need the struggle with steps tonight. As I leave I'll lock the door and drop the keys through the letterbox."

He lifted her from the sofa as she protested that she could manage. After carrying her up the narrow stairs he wished her a good night and departed. She heard the key drop to the floor and then the sound of his car leaving the cottages. As it did so there was the sound of a door banging, so she knew that Constance was home and very angry.

After she heard the car leave and the angry bang of Constance's door Helen sat on the edge of the bed and ran her mind over the events of the evening. She thought of the kind way a perfect stranger had spent time with her at the dance. He had insisted on helping her to get home, and once there had dressed her injury with gentle care. Ever since she'd been old enough to think of men and marriage she'd held to a decision she made in her early teens.

She saw unhappy marriages, and noticed the selfish attitudes of many of the lads of her own age. She hoped she would meet a man who didn't have that self-centred way with women. He'd be handsome of course, but would also be kind and share her desire for a happy marriage with lovely children. Until now there'd never been a man who seemed to fulfil her dreams, so she'd never had a steady boy friend.

Richard Moulding was handsome and she particularly liked his thick curly hair. It was a shade of brown that was almost blonde. She realised that it could turn grey later or even disappear altogether, but at present it was very attractive to her.

Her foot felt better already and she soon prepared for bed, but she didn't fall asleep immediately. She made up for this by not awakening until nearly nine o'clock. This was late for her, so she arose and dressed. She descended the stairs without too much trouble and opened the door to enjoy the beautiful morning. After a few minutes she turned and began to prepare her breakfast. She was just finishing her meal when the car that she'd come home in arrived outside her window. A few moments later there was a knock on the door and Richard came into the room.

"I didn't wait for a reply to my knock as I wasn't sure how your foot would be this morning. How's the cripple today?"

"I'm very much recovered, thank you."

"Have you put more liniment on it?"

"No, it's alright."

"Just like a woman. If there's no pain a miracle has occurred. Let me re-dress it for you."

He removed the bandage, bathed the ankle in cold water and after adding liniment replaced the bandage.

"Now you are fit enough to sit in a car and look at the scenery," he told her. "You said you were fed up with being stuck in the house unable to go anywhere or do much, so today you'll go out with me. I found a lovely beauty spot the other day that you'll be able to enjoy without walking."

After she'd got ready they had a pleasant day in a really beautiful area she'd never seen before. At a country pub they ate a simple lunch and conversed happily on various subjects. He told her he'd been ill for a lengthy period and was now close to deadlines for a couple of articles and his first novel. Nigel had given him the use of a small room without charge as he'd booked and paid for his bedroom for three months. As well as the actual writing he was also doing research for another novel he wanted to start writing as soon as the accepted one was finished.

"Is there any way that I can help you?" she asked. "I'm a fairly good typist and have no commitments."

"There's no denying that I could use a secretary for a while, but it isn't easy to work for a writer. Are you sure it wouldn't be too difficult?"

"I've never worked for an author, but I see no reason why it would be harder than legal documents, and I did plenty of those before my parents were killed, when I was able to stop working for a living."

"If you think you can help me it'll ease my position, but for this story you must be able to spell 'cat'. There's one in the first chapter."

"You must check my spelling," she replied calmly. "If I get it wrong you must fire me straight away."

"The worst thing that an author can do is be late with a promised article or story, so if you're free tomorrow I'll collect you at nine o'clock and we'll see how it goes."

At first Helen just worked on the typing, but soon she began to leave him notes about errors and possible improvements in the text.

He was amused when he saw she thought she knew how to make his work better, but soon he realised that she was often right and he began to value her opinion. Each day he collected her in the car and at lunchtime they ate a meal in the bar. Sometimes Constance was there, as she thought Nigel's wife her special friend. When she saw Helen and Richard together and learned that they were working on the book as a team she was furious. She couldn't get near him if she ignored her neighbour, and he gave her the barest of courteous greetings when they met.

Several weeks went by, and the two articles had been sent to their destinations. The work on the book was progressing steadily, and Richard was satisfied with the information he was getting for the next book. At least once every week they did no work. Instead they went out in the car to places Helen couldn't have reached without it. Her foot was getting stronger, and she was able to dance more. Many times each Friday evening she danced with Richard, and Molly began to think that she'd at last found a man who interested her more than most.

"I'll be going away on Monday," Richard told her one Friday evening as she was about to leave the car. I've to see my publisher on Tuesday, and there are personal matters later in the week. I'll write to you as soon as I know what my programme will be. I may be away as long as two weeks, but I'll keep you informed."

From somewhere Constance got hold of an out-of-date newspaper. On its front page was a photograph of a young couple. The caption was, 'Miss Doreen Nash with her fiancé Mr. R. Moulding; they are to be married next month.'

"Look at this," she said to Mrs. Holdsworth, "it'll be a nice surprise for my dear neighbour. I must make sure that she sees it."

"Do you think that you should? It sounds a bit mean if you do. Surely it'll be hard enough for her if she finds out for herself."

"The harder the better. She thinks she's perfect, and has Richard at her beck and call. She's helping with the writing and goes everywhere with him. He used to dance and talk with me until she pushed her way in. I'm going to enjoy this."

Constance may have deluded herself into thinking of Sheila Holdsworth as her special friend, but the woman had nothing but contempt for her. She told Nigel later how Constance had reacted to the photo.

"I think that she's the meanest person we get in here. I wouldn't be sorry if she never came again. Helen's a very nice person if I'm any judge of people. If this is true I'm sure that she'll be very badly hurt, and all that woman can do is gloat. She says she'll make sure that Helen will see it. I'll be surprised if there isn't an explanation as Richard is such a kind person."

Richard had written to Helen a couple of times whilst he was away, and she had replied to the address he put on the letters. Then another came telling her not to reply as he would soon be back at the hotel. When she picked up this letter there was a newspaper beside it. She unlocked the door and looked out at the sun shining on the flowers in the street.

As she didn't get a daily paper, in fact she couldn't in Harker's Bridge, she was very surprised to see it. She picked it up and casually looked at it. When she saw the picture she stopped in her steps to the table. Horrified by what she read under the photo she sank into a chair. She saw the date on the paper wasn't new.

"This is an old paper," she told herself. "He may be married by now. How could he do this to me?"

She opened his letter and read it. He was to return the day after it was posted. The wording was the same as always, except that he'd signed it 'Your Dear Friend,' a form he'd never used before.

"My dear friend is he? That's why he went away, not to see his publisher but to marry this woman. He said there was some personal matter, now I know what it was. How could he do this to me?"

She put her head down on the table and wept bitterly. All her hopes and dreams were shattered. He'd never really suggested that he was having thoughts of love for her, but as they worked and relaxed together it was inevitable that she would think he considered her special. When she was helping him with the writing and when they were in the bar or out in the car they had always been in perfect harmony. He'd shown kindness and concern over her injury and given the impression that he wanted her company, just the opposite of his remarks about Constance.

As she sat weeping she seemed to realise that she wasn't alone. She raised her head and saw Richard standing beside her.

"Whatever is the matter?" he asked when he saw the flushed face and the tears running down her cheeks.

"Well may you ask! You told me you weren't married and have spent all these weeks taking me out in your car, and when I was helping you with the book you treated me as if I meant something to you. I know you never made me any promises or told me I was special to you, but any woman would have thought as I did, that you were beginning to want me in your life. Why did you treat me like that when there was another woman in your plans?"

As she spoke Richard noticed the newspaper on the floor. The front page was uppermost so he picked it up. "Is it this that has upset you? Do you think this is me?"

"Of course it is. The caption says that's you. Where is she? I suppose you were with her when you sent me this last letter to break my heart. How could I fail to think you were in love with me when I saw how you closed it?" She indicated the words above his signature, 'I just can't wait to be with you again.' "How could you write that when you were with her? The way that you spoke to me and treated me these many weeks have made me love you. You must have enjoyed the conquest of a woman who'd never loved anyone except her father."

"Yes, I've been where Doreen was, after I finished my visit to my publisher. It was her wedding, but she didn't marry me. That man in the picture isn't me, it's my cousin Roland. We're doubles, and if you ever meet our fathers you'll see that they're very much alike. How did you get this paper?"

"It was on the mat this morning with the letter."

"In that case we know who sent it and why. The horrid hag, to play a trick like that. Somewhere she must have seen it, and she pushed it through your door."

"Oh, Richard, is that true this is your cousin and not you? This has really upset me this morning."

"Yes it's true. Roland and Doreen were married last Saturday and are now in Edinburgh on their honeymoon. I think I know how you can make that woman wish that she hadn't done this. We can book the hall for our wedding reception, invite some of the residents of the valley, and publicly bar Constance from the room. I'll have a word with Nigel about it and show him the paper. Of course there's only one thing that could spoil it."

"What's that?"

"You may not want to marry me, I haven't asked you yet."

"I can't refuse you until you do."

"Will you marry me, Helen? I've wanted to tell you how much I've come to love you, but I waited until I was sure the book was sold. Now I know, and have the advance cheque in my pocket. I know now I'll be able to keep a wife in the way I should. Please say 'Yes', Helen."

"Yes, I must marry you now. If I don't I can't see any other way to make that woman squirm after what she's done this morning. Besides, I've already said you've made me love you."

"Thank you, darling, I'll try to make you happy. I must make arrangements for us to visit my family, but we'll wait until Roland and Doreen return to Devon. My cousin is very dear to me, as are all of my family. We're a very close knit bunch and you'll be part of it soon."

"Will we work on your book today?"

"I think we have something else to attend to first. Get ready, we're going to Leeds to get a ring. We'll have lunch there; if we get back in time we'll check my mail. There'll be a lot after I've been away so long, so I doubt if we'll get anything else done."

Helen soon prepared for the journey, and they were away by ten o'clock. She was happy and wondered how she could have believed that Richard would treat her so badly, but that was all over and she determined to put it behind her. When they arrived in the city Richard parked the car in a side street. They spent a long time walking from one jeweller to another, looking in their windows at the beautiful rings on display. When they'd visited most of the shops in the centre Helen saw a ring she really liked.

"Richard, look at this one with the emerald. It's lovely, but far too expensive for us."

"Don't worry about the price. Under my bed is a special box with a label on it, 'Money to be spent on Helen'."

"Don't be silly, I know you aren't as daft as that. I do like it though."

"I only intend to buy one engagement ring, so it must be a good one. A special one for a special lady. Come on inside."

The salesman lifted from the window the tray on which the desired ring was displayed. They examined it carefully and Helen tried it on. It fitted perfectly without any adjustment and Helen was ecstatic when Richard wrote out the cheque and gave proof of his identity because of the high price of the ring. After a telephone call to the bank the manager allowed them to take home the ring, and also provided temporary insurance for it.

"I act as agent for this company because many of our customers wish to cover any risk on the way home. We like to see sensible precautions being taken, and it's a simple service for us to provide."

When they left the shop it was lunchtime, so they found a restaurant with a menu that satisfied their needs. Richard had put the box containing the ring in his pocket; when they were settled at their table he took it out and removed the ring.

"Miss Field, are you still willing to marry me?"

"Would I be sensible if I refused when you're holding a lovely ring like that?"

"Does that mean 'Yes'? I need to be sure before I put it on your hand," Richard said with a twinkle in his eye.

"Yes, Mr. Moulding, I'll marry you at the first opportunity if you'll promise me another ring for that same day."

"I'll do that, you gold digger," he promised as he took her left hand and placed the ring on her finger. Helen turned her hand in every direction to catch the light on the lovely green stone. Richard watched his fiancé and enjoyed her happiness.

"I feel really ashamed about this morning," she told him. "How could I have doubted you?"

"Quite easily, it was set up with that photograph to hurt you, and we know the guilty person. I'm not surprised you fell for it. We haven't known each other a very long time you know. I'm not sorry it happened, as it gave me an opportunity to ask you to marry me. It isn't the easiest thing to do, because unless the moment is right the lady may resist."

After the meal they decided to return to Foxton.

"We'll call in the bar if it's still open," Helen said. "William will be on duty as its Percy's day off. Who knows, Miss Constance Manning will perhaps be there too, and I'm sure that she'll be delighted to see this beauty."

They had a speedy journey home, and after parking the car they entered the bar. It was only 2.30, so it was still open and William was there. His only customer was Constance. He was helping the porter with some bottles to avoid having to talk to her.

"Hello," he greeted the couple. "I don't often see you two at this hour, you're usually gone before this."

"We haven't been working. We went to Leeds, and now I've made Richard come in so that I can show you the lovely ring he's bought me. I wanted one of your family to be the first to see it."

For the next few minutes William and the porter admired the bright green stone and its setting and congratulated the lovers. Constance was looking blackly as she realised that her scheme hadn't worked, and instead of parting the couple were now committed to each other. She rapped sharply on the bar top.

"Is it possible for a customer to have some attention, or do I have to seek out the manager and complain?"

"Complain if you wish, Miss Manning, but it'll do you no good. What are you requiring?"

"Civility from the staff of this establishment, and some service. As you may have observed, if you've found time to finish with those people, my glass has been empty for a considerable time and I wish to have it refilled."

"Yes, it's nearly been one minute," William observed as he put a double gin in the glass and a small bottle of tonic water beside it. "I know you don't like Miss Field, though I can't imagine why, but don't start trouble here. They're celebrating their engagement, if you try to spoil it I'll be the one to complain to Mr. Holdsworth."

Just then Sheila Holdsworth entered the bar with a cup of tea for William.

"Sheila, will you tell that barman I'm a regular customer and should be treated as one?"

"Why, what's wrong?"

"Those people came in, and he was so busy making a fuss of them that I had to complain because I couldn't get a drink. He then became most uncivil."

"That's not the truth," Richard said. "When we came in Helen showed William her engagement ring and we chatted about it for a few moments. That woman hates Helen, and I suspect it was her who put through her door a paper with a photo of my cousin with the woman who is now his wife. As he's my double it caused her great distress, as I found out when I returned from the wedding.

"This afternoon she again tried to destroy Helen's happiness and hurt William by threatening to complain to Nigel. In no way did William do or say anything but what any competent barman would do."

"That's true, Mrs. Holdsworth," the porter said as he straightened from putting the last of the bottles on the bottom shelf. "We both admired the ring and congratulated them, then Miss Manning tried to spoil things."

"If you believe any of that you're as bad as them," Constance declared. "You're supposed to be my friend, so do something about that fellow. Tell Nigel to sack him. As for what Mr. Moulding said, it's all a pack of lies."

"Now look here, Constance, let us get a few things straight," Sheila ordered. "First, I'm no more your friend than that of any well behaved customer. Secondly, William is a first class barman, though he still lacks experience in some areas, mainly dealing with awkward customers. Thirdly, it's no use saying that Mr. Moulding is lying. You showed me that paper with the photograph in it, and laughed at what it would do to Miss Field. I'll tell Nigel, but it'll not be William whom I suggest he gets rid of."

Sheila then turned to Helen, "May I see your ring?"

"Of course."

The landlady came along the bar and examined the jewel. "That is really lovely, and it's the right colour for your hair and complexion. Congratulations to both of you. When will the wedding take place?"

"We're not sure yet," Richard told her. "We'll be going down to Barnstaple for a couple of weeks for her to meet my people, including the man that woman tried to use against us. Then we'll have to arrange the ceremony, and book your hall and rooms for my family. We don't intend to wait long."

As they finished their drinks Sheila sent the porter to fetch a bottle of champagne and call Nigel.

What's the matter?" he asked when he came into the room.

"Nothing now. We're celebrating. You're to pour the champagne because Richard and Helen are going to get married. Look at that lovely ring."

Nigel admired it and poured out seven glasses of the wine. He handed one each to Helen and Richard, one each to his wife, William and the porter. He began to take the last one to Constance but she stopped him.

"I don't want one. I won't drink to that bitch's happiness."

"Whoah, what's all this about?" Nigel asked.

"Constance has caused Helen distress at home with a photo of Richard's cousin, and she wants you to sack William. She seems to hate all who live near her."

"Except Jean Baker," William added. "She gave support to Jean's slanderous attack a while ago."

"She mustn't bring her hatred in here," Nigel declared. He turned to Constance, "Apologise to Miss Field for what you have just called her."

"Not likely."

"Then leave the premises and don't come back. We don't need trouble makers here. There's been enough fighting in these recent years without us having it here. That war is over, and you'll not start another here."

Constance glared at Nigel but didn't move to leave. Instead she put her glass on the bar and began fumbling in her purse for money.

"Please refill my glass," she politely requested of William.

"You heard Mr. Holdsworth, I can't serve you unless you apologise to Miss Field."

"Then I'll not come here again, and I'll tell my friends to stay away as well."

"The Bakers aren't our customers, and I haven't heard that you have other friends, so we'll not lose much," William said quietly as she stormed out of the building.

"For once I'm glad that we've no other customers here," Nigel remarked. "I hope that she does stay away, in fact she'll have to unless she apologises to you, Helen. She may try to come to the dances, but it applies to the whole building. She can say and do what she likes as far as I'm concerned when she's in Harker's Bridge, but on my property no woman will be called a bitch."

"I've no idea why she hates me so much," Helen said.

"She's jealous," William told her. "You have friends, and now you've won Richard. She only has Jean Baker. She always claimed that Sheila was her friend, but now she knows differently. Don't let her spoil your day."

About ten days later Richard wrote to his parents, and it was arranged he would take Helen to Barnstaple for two weeks. She'd never seen Devonshire, so apart from her desire to meet Richard's family she was eager to see the county. On the day they left Harker's Bridge for the long journey the sun was shining and the air was warm, but not too hot for the drive to be comfortable.

"I hope it'll be like this all the way," Richard commented. "I don't like driving in rain, and this is a long journey. We're in no hurry, so we'll find a nice place for lunch and spend the night in Gloucester. Tomorrow we'll leave there about ten, and be in Barnstaple in the late afternoon. It's a pity you aren't a driver; I'll have to teach you."

Throughout the trip Helen found the scenery interesting. She had never been out of West Yorkshire so the changes between hills and flatter country, arable land and that used for dairy farms was all new to her. On her arrival at Barnstaple she was delighted by the small town.

As Richard stopped the car outside his parents' home his mother opened the door of the thatched cottage. She was a smallish lady with short grey hair and spectacles. The lovers got out of the car, collected their luggage from the back seat, and Richard locked the doors.

"Hello, Mother, this is Helen, the prize I won in Yorkshire."

"Welcome to Barnstaple, Helen," the older lady said as she put her arms around her. "Come inside, you must both be tired after that long drive."

"We've only been on the road since 10.30, and we stopped for lunch," her son told her. "We spent the night in Gloucester to break the journey."

As they entered the old house Richard's father arose from his chair. He greeted his son warmly and was introduced to Helen.

"Now, young lady, what do you intend to do with that son of mine? He can be a bit of a problem sometimes."

"I like solving problems," she replied with a smile. "I know he's a very kind and gentle person. The first time we met he helped me a lot."

"Richard, you've a loyal fan here. What did you do to get a recommendation like that?"

"I simply used my car to help a lady in pain to get home."

Helen looked on the two men and liked what she saw. The older one seemed to be around the lower fifties, and he was slightly shorter than his son. His hair was grey, and there were some grey hairs in the brown moustache that he wore. He had on a woollen cardigan and a pair of flannel trousers with a pale blue shirt.

"Come and sit down, Mother will have a cup of tea ready soon."

This cheerful welcome told Helen that she'd enjoy her stay here, and that her lover's people were welcoming her into the family as well as their home. As the evening progressed the older couple noticed her quiet manner and thought that they would probably like her. Mrs. Moulding tried to assess her as a wife for her son; like most mothers she was concerned for his future happiness. After the meal and a period of conversation Richard suggested to Helen they should go for a short walk.

"We've been stuck in that car for the last two days. Let me show you the river. There's a fine long row of elms on one side of the path with the river on the other, with green hills behind. I think you'll like it, and your young friend George would be fascinated by the bird life."

They walked along the wide path between the elms and the Tay. Birds and men were fishing in the cool of the evening as they found a seat on which to sit and enjoy the fresh air and each other.

"Your parents seemed to accept me." Helen said.

"Of course they did. I told them in a letter how wonderful you are."

After about half an hour of this kind of conversation they set off back towards the town and Helen noticed the bridge for the first time.

"What a lovely view. With the sun beginning to sink, the bridge and the gleam of the water further downstream, it's lovely. I'm going to enjoy this fortnight. I like this clock tower as well."

"It's called the Albert Clock, after Prince Albert, I think. That means it's probably well over a hundred years old. Yes, this is a beautiful place, and I'll show you other parts of the county, but we'll take it easy tomorrow and meet my cousin and his wife. Then you'll wonder which is me, but if you make a mistake Doreen will chase you off. She says Roland is nicer, but I don't think that can be true."

When they returned to the cottage Richard told his parents the outline plan for the wedding. As they were going to marry in Yorkshire the Devonshire contingent would stay in the hotel.

"It's a long way, we'll come by train," his father said. "I don't want to drive all that way in my little car. I don't know what Roland and Doreen will do. They won't have much petrol left after their wedding."

"As you've no relatives able to be there why can't you be married here?" Mrs. Moulding asked.

"I've two families of neighbours who were wonderful to me when I'd to stay off my foot some months ago. They both have children, but I specially want them at my wedding. I needed all the help that I could get, and they were wonderful in ways that Richard couldn't have been if we'd known each other then."

"In that case you're right to have it there," the hostess agreed. "Friends are scarce, and if you get a real one you should be a friend in return."

"We'll find out Roland's plan tomorrow as we're going to see them. Helen needs to know only I am me, all others are fakes. Someone got hold of a picture of Roland with Doreen in an old newspaper and tried to upset Helen by putting it through her door. The trick worked, but I arrived just in time to put it right. It cost me a ring though."

As both the young people were tired Richard said he'd crawl to his old room, and his mother led Helen to a nice bedroom that looked on a view of the Taw and the hills beyond. Next morning Richard and Helen got into the car and drove a few miles to a cottage by the sea. It had a small front garden full of roses and a vegetable and fruit area round the back. Richard stopped the car and tooted the horn.

A slim, dark young lady came to the door and Helen recognised her as the young woman in the photograph. Behind her was the exact double of Richard, and a small terrier bounced out between them to be the first to interview the visitors.

"Hello, Judy," Richard said as he petted the animal. "Hello to you two as well. I've brought the loveliest flower in Yorkshire for you to see. Her name is Helen." He turned to his companion, "This is Doreen, and here is the man you thought was me, my cousin Roland."

They all happily joined in conversation as they went indoors.

"How did Helen think that I was you? She's never met me before, and in any case I'm much more handsome."

"That last part isn't true." He told them what had happened. "I don't know how the woman got a local paper from here, unless someone had taken it to the hotel and left it there. You nearly lost me my girl. I just got back in time as the caption said Mr. R. Moulding and mentioned your forthcoming wedding."

"Oh I remember, the local paper had a photo of us about a month ago," Doreen said.

"So you've brought her down to prove your integrity?" Roland suggested. "Be careful, Helen, he's a dark horse, or should I say a black sheep?"

"Now cut the nonsense and let me tell you your duty, cousin. We'll be getting married soon, and I want you to be the best man."

"You want us to go all the way to Yorkshire to help condemn that poor girl to a life with you? I'm not sure that I should be a party to such a crime."

"Will it be half as bad as what I did to Doreen a few weeks ago?"

When the cousins stopped teasing each other Doreen promised that they would be there no matter when the ceremony took place. Conversation became general, and the two cousins planned a basic programme for Helen to see as much as possible of the county. Helen and Doreen took a liking for each other very quickly, and the four young people enjoyed the day together.

"I hope you'll bring her again before you go back north," Doreen told Richard.

"That'll depend on how much we're able to explore the county," he replied. "She's never been to Devon before."

"Never?" Doreen cried. "Girl, you've never lived."

With those words ringing in their ears the lovers left for the return to Richard's parents' home.

CHAPTER 8

Helen and Richard walked into the bar where William was working. Nigel was also there.

"Good morning, gentlemen," Richard greeted them.

"Good morning," Nigel replied.

William put their drinks on the bar and took the food order.

"How're you two on this lovely day?" he asked.

"We're fine," Richard told him before turning to Nigel. "When you've some spare time we'd like to talk with you."

"Certainly, what can I do for you?"

"We want a date when two of your rooms will be available other than mine. We'll need them for seven nights, starting on a Monday. We'll also need William for an afternoon and evening."

"I'll go fetch my book and see what's available. What're you planning to do, or should I know?"

"Perhaps you do," Helen said. "When this man put a ring on my finger he promised that he would bring another on a future date. This will be the occasion that I'm expecting."

Nigel left the bar and returned a few minutes later with a large book. He studied its contents for a few moments.

"How soon will you want the rooms?"

"Any time in May or June will do. As I said we'll need them for seven days, starting Monday. There'll not be very many of us, so a part of the restaurant will be large enough for the reception. This will be on the Saturday after my relatives arrive. They will travel on Mondays to avoid the weekend repairs and maintenance on the railways. They're coming on a long enough journey without those delays. Now the snow has at last all gone they can come north without freezing to death on stations. The main problem is tying the wedding to the availability of your rooms."

Nigel studied his book. "I can offer you three dates in late May and June when there'll be rooms available as you need them. If you can arrange the wedding for one of them we'll be able to fix it up immediately."

"That'll be fine. We've spoken to the minister at Cottley chapel. If you give me your dates I'll telephone him and make final arrangements."

Nigel wrote down on a piece of paper the three dates that were free and Richard went to make the call.

"I've booked the chapel for the first Saturday in June," he told the others when he returned a few minutes later. "The ceremony will be at three o'clock. That gives us nearly five weeks for everyone to make their arrangements."

"That's fine," Nigel told him as he noted the booking. "You included William in the original statement of your needs. I'd have thought you'd have wanted this top class barman on duty that day."

"Apart from the toasts there will be very little drink needed. None of us are heavy drinkers. The point of the matter is Helen wants the Briggs family as guests."

"I certainly do. I don't know how I'd have managed without them and Nora Donovan when I was injured. Richard's mother suggested we should marry in Barnstaple, but although I've no close relatives who'll be able to come I want my best friends there. Young Doris Slater was a good help too, so I'll ask her if she'd like to be my bridesmaid."

"In that case we must let him have the day off. I'll arrange it."

"Mother will be half gone on one small glass of champagne," Richard said, "and none of the others drink much. We're a family who like to enjoy our food and drink in moderation and give full attention to the company we're with."

During the following weeks the Moulding family made their plans and bookings for the journey to Yorkshire. Helen and Richard sent out the invitations and other arrangements were completed. Doris was delighted when she was asked to be the bridesmaid. She'd never been to a wedding. Her father had died when Doris was a baby so Helen invited her mother as well.

Helen and Sheila planned the meal together. Though she didn't really expect her to accept Helen invited Alice Shepherd because she and George were so close. To George's delight she accepted. Of course Molly, Helen's dancing friend, would be there. This made a total of sixteen people to cater for including the bride and groom.

Gradually the preparations were completed. Helen's and Doris' dresses were ordered and delivered. The cake was made by the head bakeress of a catering firm, and delivered to the hotel in time for the wedding. The taxi was booked, and Nigel assured them all would be fed. There would be champagne, and for the children soft drinks would be provided in variety. Mr. Shepherd told George that although he wouldn't be staying for the reception he'd get Alice to the chapel, and stay to take her and anyone else to the hotel afterwards.

The meal would be in the restaurant, and Richard arranged with the promoter of the dances that the programme for the evening would be 50/50, so that older people would enjoy the Viennese type and those wanting ballroom wouldn't be left out. He also arranged passes for all his party to use as they wished during the evening. As both he and Helen were regular attenders at the dances and they had met at one of them the man was very happy to oblige.

When it seemed to Helen the preparations were never going to be ready in time the day came when a taxi brought the Mouldings from the railway station to the hotel. Helen was with her fiancé to greet them. It was a glorious afternoon.

"Did you have a pleasant journey?" Richard asked his cousin.

"Yes, it was very interesting. None of us had ever been so far north. As you know I was in the Navy, and I saw a lot of the Mediterranean lands, but all this is strange to me."

"Come inside," Richard told them when the taxi had left and greetings had been exchanged. "Prepare for dinner at six, and there's no need to dress formally. You've about two hours."

"In that case I'd like a cup of tea now," his mother told him. "We had a drink on the train, but that was a long time ago."

Helen went to order the tea and cakes, and it was Nigel himself who brought them. As this was the first wedding catered for since the place was extended he wanted everything to go perfectly, especially on the day of the wedding. He was introduced to the newcomers.

"We want you to enjoy your stay with us," he told them. There are two reasons for this. We want you to tell those poor people in Devon what they are missing if they don't come to Yorkshire and stay at my hotel. The other reason is that Helen will kill me very cruelly if you don't enjoy being here."

As they'd all met Helen in Barnstaple the Mouldings were anxious to see her on her home ground. Richard's mother was especially interested as anyone can be nice for a few days as a guest, but in their own environment people show their true nature so much more clearly. She was pleased by what she saw, and as in her own home, she felt that Richard had made a good choice.

The two hours before dinner sped very quickly. The wives unpacked the cases and hung the suits and dresses in the wardrobes whilst Roland and Mr. Moulding Senior told Richard news of friends in Devon. When the ladies rejoined them the programme for the week was outlined. Richard's car had only two seats so Nigel offered to lend them his larger vehicle that could carry six, so they could tour the area together.

After the meal the party adjourned to the private lounge, a small room that had been added when the alterations were done. Drinks were ordered and brought to them by William, who was introduced by Helen.

"This man and his family live in the cottage next to mine. They were more than friends when I was injured, just before Richard and I met for the first time. They are part of the reason why I want the ceremony here. Apart from one of his sons who's in the forces he and his family and other people who helped me will be at the wedding."

When 10 o'clock came the travellers decided it was time to think about bed, so Richard got out his car and took Helen home before he also retired for the night.

Throughout the following days the priority was to finalise the preparations for the wedding. Only important communications from the publisher were allowed to take precedence over them, and there weren't many of those. Minor adjustments to Doris' dress had been made, and both were taken to Helen's cottage ready for use. The pale yellow of the girl's dress really looked well with her young features and black hair.

Richard wanted his family to see as much of the beauty of Yorkshire as possible whilst they were there, so he took them to York where his mother was impressed by the architecture of the Minster. At Haworth all were fascinated by the story of the Bronte sisters and the difficulties they overcame to produce their wonderful books. The weather behaved kindly all week, so they had plenty of opportunity to see the beauty of the Dales and compare it with the grimness of Dartmoor.

+ + +

Saturday morning arrived, and Helen was awake soon after the sun rose. She couldn't sleep and was restless, so she got out of bed and dressed. This was the day she'd dreamed about for a long time, wondering if it would ever come. When she first met Richard a faint hope began to develop, today that hope would become reality. By tonight she'd be a married woman, her name would change and a new life would be ahead of her. Her excitement was only controlled by her determination to play her part in the wedding ceremony in a dignified and proper manner.

She made her breakfast, and as she ate it she thought of Richard's goodnight kiss only a few hours previously. Tonight he wouldn't kiss and leave, he would kiss and stay with her for the rest of their lives. As she thought how lovely that would be she determined that whatever circumstances came in their life together she would always try her utmost to care for, love and respect the wonderful man she was to marry in a few hours time.

The morning seemed to be endless. As she had risen so early she had eaten her breakfast long before most of her neighbours were awake. She decided to take a walk in the woods and listen to the birds singing. This was always a pleasure for her, and as she sat on a rock listening to a song thrush she found herself wishing that Richard was sharing it with her.

"Next time I hear that bird he'll be here with me," she thought.

At 1.30pm Gwen and Nora came to get her ready. Shortly afterwards Doris and her mother, whose name was Gladys, arrived and the cottage was a hive of activity. The three older ladies worked on the two younger ones, preparing them for their part in the forefront of the afternoon's events. Gladys was a trained hair dresser. In recent years she'd only practised on the ladies of the valley, but she hadn't forgotten any of her skill. She worked on both her daughter and the bride as soon as the others were satisfied with the dresses.

The bouquets had been delivered earlier, and by the time the taxi arrived all was ready. Just before it stopped outside the house Roland Moulding came to collect Gwen and Gladys. Nora and the twins had already left on Pat's motorbike and sidecar.

At the chapel Richard and his cousin were in their seats by 2.45. As he had recently married Roland was wearing the light brown suit he'd chosen for that occasion. Richard had on a navy blue three piece suit new from the tailor, and both had white carnations in their lapels. George Briggs was outside the chapel waiting for the arrival of the bride's taxi. He was happy when he saw Alice arrive with her father.

"Alice, you look lovely," he told her. "You must be careful or Richard may mistake you for the bride and marry you. What would I do then?"

"I've a shotgun I can lend you," Walter told him.

"No, they use them to make men marry, not to stop them," George said with a laugh. "Just you guard her for me until I get the real bride into the building."

As his fiancé went into the chapel with her father George noticed the taxi coming up the street. He gave the signal to the organist who stopped playing the piece she was using and started the Wedding March. Helen and Doris walked to the front of the room with William who was to give the bride away.

At exactly three o'clock the minister came from the vestry to face the cousins. He hadn't yet got used to their being doubles, so he checked they were standing in the right places.

"We don't want Mr. Roland to marry again and have two wives, leaving you with none," he told Richard to settle his nerves. Fortunately that didn't happen, and the marriage took place without a hitch.

When all the legal formalities had been dealt with, and the official photographer was satisfied that he had used enough film, Roland took the bride and groom to the hotel where they would receive their guests. He then returned to collect the Slaters and Gwen and William. Walter gathered Alice, George and Molly, as well as Sheila who hurried indoors as soon as they arrived to oversee the staff.

The meal was served in one half of the restaurant and all settled down to enjoy it. In his Best Man's speech Roland began by commenting on it.

"I must begin by complimenting the management for feeding us so well. Weddings are a very good way for a man to get enough to eat in these days of rationing. I also want to commend the bride for her bravery, but I have a warning for her. Mrs. Moulding, the latest, for there are now three of you, you're a very brave woman. I know our Richard, strange as that may seem to some of you, and he's a good man, but he has a fault. He's older than I am and until I managed to grow as big as him he bullied me terribly. Beware, Helen, you have been warned."

He then turned to Doris, "Miss Slater, since I found that I could eat well at weddings I've been to many. I don't go to see the bride, but to obtain my favourite food, fruit cake. However, I always notice the bridesmaids, but I've never seen one who looked lovelier than you did today. If I didn't have to check that our Richard did his job properly with that ring I would never have seen the bride.

"I understand that there's a dance downstairs tonight, and some of us are going to end the evening there. As Best Man I claim a dance with the Bridesmaid as compensation for having to control my cousin in the chapel."

Doris was thrilled when he ended the speech by calling for a toast for her. She certainly enjoyed her first time at a wedding.

Helen too was very happy. Later she managed to have a few words with Alice.

"I'm very glad you came today," she said after Alice had thanked her for the invitation. "I know George will enjoy the evening more with you here. Everyone has done his or her best to make this the happiest day of my life. My only regret is that my sister Margaret was unable to be here. It's a very long journey and she has commitments that make it very difficult for her to be away from home over the weekend. Richard and the Holdsworths have arranged everything so well that I'm really happy."

"I'm glad for you. I hope when we marry everything will go as well for us. Even the weather has been marvellous, allowing the Mouldings to see some of our county in the best conditions. We're glad for you, but also for ourselves. George has never been invited to a wedding before. Now he'll have some idea what we'll need on our day, whenever that will be."

"Yes, and I must congratulate you on being engaged to a fine man. He's the second nicest man I know. I have the nicest."

"That's a matter of opinion and I can't agree," Alice said with a smile.

"Have you any idea when you'll marry?"

"Not yet. Officially we aren't engaged, but I think everyone knows the situation. It's very difficult to arrange anything when we don't know what the Government and the armed forces will demand. At least they've let him finish his education. He may get called up like others, but now the war is over they could demand that he uses his high qualifications in French and German to help sort out the mess Hitler has made of Europe. They say that the German population is almost starving. We can't plan our lives until we know what will be decided."

"I suppose he'll want to wait until he has a job with a decent salary."
"We want that, but finance won't stop us when other things are right. Dad is planning to retire, as he sees the small textile mills' days are ending. He's

promised both Ernest and us a definite sum to get us started, then it'll be up to us. Ernest has been offered a good position in a big mill in Bingley and he's getting married soon. For us it's just the uncertainty of the immediate future. If they do send him to Germany to use his linguistic skills it'll be a good step towards a better post in Civvy Street. We'll just have to wait and hope."

"One thing I'm sure about, he's worth waiting for."

"I know that, I really love him, and he's taught me so much about nature that we've a common interest outside the home that'll be an added strength for our marriage."

"Yes, and I'm sure that he's as much in love as you are. His mother is one of my best friends, and she tells me things."

"When we do marry I hope that you and Richard will be able to be there."

Later in the evening the weekly dance started and the group moved down to it. Mrs. Moulding was rather tired, so it wasn't long before she went to bed. Nora and Pat took their boys home soon afterwards, but all the others stayed to the end. Doris was thrilled when Roland came for his dance, and it was her first dance at a public affair. Most of the people there knew Richard and Helen, so the evening seemed more like an extension of their reception.

When it was all over Richard took Molly home, then all those for Harkers' Bridge. He wouldn't let Roland drive as he wasn't used to the twisting lanes after dark. Finally he and Helen were alone in the room he'd occupied so long. They'd postponed leaving on a honeymoon until Monday, after his relations left on the long journey south.

Once they'd left in a taxi, waved away by Nigel, Sheila and all of their staff, the same sort of farewell was accorded to the newlyweds as they left for a week in Scotland, with a hope of visiting Margaret so that she could meet Richard. When they returned after fulfilling that hope they settled in Helen's cottage. It had been agreed that Richard would continue to use the room in the hotel for his writing until he managed to obtain a small office, as the cottage was so small.

CHAPTER 9

The year after Helen's wedding Alice looked out of the kitchen window and saw the sun shining on the fields. She'd been helping her mother with the housework as she did two days each week. The other three she worked for her father in the mill office, then had the weekend for herself.

"Is there anything else you wish to do today, Mum?"

"No, I think we've done enough for today, apart from preparing food as always. Women have never finished, there's always something wants doing, but we've done enough for today."

"In that case I'll walk down to the hide. It's a lovely day, and we have a pair of grebes on the dam. They are very funny in their courtship, I love to watch them."

"Alright, but be careful, and make sure that nobody is lurking nearby."

"I'll be fine, mother. The hide is out in the open where there are no trees. George built it on this side of the dam and it's not far from the mill."

She picked up her binoculars and walked down the short slope to the dam. Various birds were singing as it was April, the height of the nesting season. She entered the small hide and began to look out to see what might be on the water. She expected George to be home during the next couple of days for the Easter break. It would be nice if the weather held and the sun shone as it was doing then, so that they could watch the birds together.

As she looked out she noticed several mallards and a pair of coots near the banks. In the middle the two grebes were bobbing and shaking their heads and presenting pieces of vegetation to each other. She was fascinated as she watched their display. She listened to the various songbirds, and was able to identify most of them. George was a good teacher, and she was an eager pupil.

She compared the peace of the dam and its surroundings with the noise and bustle on the other side of the walls of the mill. On the days when she worked in her father's office she hated having to pass between the machines when they were working.

She was intently watching a treecreeper on an oak on the far side of the water. As she adjusted her binoculars she heard a slight sound behind her. Perhaps George had come home already and had come to see the grebes she had told him about in a letter. She turned her head to greet him, but it wasn't her friend who stood in the doorway of the hide. Wilfred Baker was only three feet away and looking hungrily at her.

"Wilfred, what are you doing here? This is private land."

"I know, but it's not too private for George Briggs. He comes here with you. I may have been in Africa and other dangerous places, but I know what's going on in the valley. Now I'm home for a while, so you can spend some time with me."

"No, Wilfred, I won't. George does come here, but he got my father's permission. He built this hide so that we can watch the birds and other wild life. He's taught me a lot about them. It's quiet and peaceful here, and we want it to stay that way, so neither you nor anyone else can come. As I said before, this is private land."

"Yes, I know George taught you about the birds, and I suppose he taught you about other things as well. I've been fighting Germans, so I've a right to a share of what he's been getting. I'll soon find out if he's as good a teacher about that as the other."

"What do you mean?"

"This. Give me a kiss to start with." He took two steps forward and threw an arm around her neck, and with the other hand grabbed roughly at her breast. He brought his face close to try to kiss her.

Alice screamed and tried to free herself, but Wilfred had grown tall like his mother. Army training and the privations of war had made him strong and powerful, and even more brutal than he'd been at school. As she struggled he gripped even more firmly on her breast, and her dress was badly ripped.

"Get off me, you brute," she shouted. "Help me someone."

A man burst into the hide.

"I will," he said as he landed a rain of blows on the face of the soldier.

Blood spurted from Wilfred's nose, and both his lips were cut. He had military training in unarmed combat, but both his hands were occupied when the attack began, and he never had a chance to defend himself. He was beaten before he had them free. His eyebrow was badly cut and was bleeding enough to temporarily blind one eye. He let go of Alice and tried to defend himself but, the onslaught continued. Another hard blow to the side of his head sent him crashing into one of the posts that formed the frame of the hide, and he received further damage.

"That's enough, George, he's not worth killing," Ernest said as he pulled the angry avenger off his victim.

"Thank God you came when you did," Alice told her friend. "He was going to rape me. He said he was going to enjoy what you were getting, and that he wanted to see if you'd taught me other things as well as about the birds. I didn't know that you'd arrived home."

"I only got here a couple of hours ago. I'd a bite to eat, then came to see the grebes you wrote about. Instead I saw a vicious animal attacking you. It's a good job you arrived when you did, Ernest, or I might have done too much."

"What do we do with this vermin?" Ernest asked as his father entered the hide.

"What's been happening? Why were you screaming, Alice?"

"Because I didn't want to be raped, Dad. Look at this dress."

"Did he do that?" her father asked as he indicated Wilfred.

"Yes, and if George hadn't arrived he'd have done a lot more. He seemed to think that George and I do other things beside watching birds, and he said he wanted the same."

"Well, why not? Why is it always the Briggs lot who get things?" I've been fighting for my country and he gets the fun with the girl. I like fun with girls as much as any Briggs swine."

"Don't you class my sister with the scum women who would entertain you or I'll give you another beating. My sister is a lady."

"Yes they all are until you get them alone. Briggs will know how ladylike she is when they get together."

"One more remark like that and you'll get the beating I threatened to give you. I'm a lot bigger than George so beware. Now get off our land and never come back."

As there were now three men beside himself in the hide Wilfred took the opportunity to escape. He staggered as he walked and Walter was alarmed.

"We need to keep an eye on him, we don't want him to fall into the dam and drown."

"Why not?" his son asked

"Because he would frighten my grebes and George hasn't seen then yet," Alice said. "Besides, a thing like that would poison the fish."

"You should go back to the mill, son," Walter told Ernest. "I left Jim in charge, but we mustn't leave him too long. George, will you see Alice home? She needs to get that dress off."

"Certainly, Mr. Shepherd."

+ + +

"Alice, whatever has happened to you?" Mrs. Shepherd asked when the two young people came into the house.

"I was attacked by Wilfred Baker. George arrived just in time to stop him from raping me. You should see his face. I would never have thought of George as a fighter."

"I'm not, but when I saw him hurting you I saw red."

"Come with me, Alice, we must get that dress off. You cannot stand there holding it all the time."

"I know, mother, I feel awful and naked."

"It's not your fault," George told her. "Don't throw the dress away. If I know his mother we may have more trouble with them, because she thinks that he's perfect. I certainly made a mess of his face; that dress shows that I'd just cause."

A few minutes later the ladies returned to the kitchen where George was waiting.

"Now we'll all have a cup of tea and we'll feel better," Mrs. Shepherd said.

"I'll make it, Mother, I need something to do. We all knew that Wilfred was evil, but I never thought that he would come to the hide, especially when the mill is working so close to it. With all the windows open both Dad and Ernest heard me scream. They came, but I don't think it would have been in time. I'll never forget how you rescued me, George."

"I know that we're only supposed to be bird watchers," George said, "but you mean a lot to me. I'd have tried to help any girl in those circumstances, but I doubt if I'd have been so fierce. I never even stopped to think. If I had done the yellow streak down my back would have shone like the sun. In some things I'm a bit of a coward."

"You're no coward to face a big brute like Wilfred," Alice replied. "He was bad enough before, but now he's been in the army seven years. His viciousness is even worse because he's been trained how to use it. If he's out of the army now it looks as if we're stuck with him again."

Alice poured three cups of tea, and her mother produced three biscuits,

"I don't think you two are just birdwatchers, George," she said. "My husband and I aren't so stupid. I believe he's intimated that he's not against you thinking of a future together, and neither am I. Of course we could be wrong, but it seems to us that you're both very keen to be together, even when there are no birds. Today has shown me that you are worthy to be her man, if that's what you both want."

"When our family came here for tea four years ago Ernest asked me my intentions, and I told him if I'm able to get a good job with a proper salary and Alice is still single I'll ask her to marry me. That still holds, but I don't think that she ever knew of that conversation until now. I'll leave university in July, and I expect to do so with honours. It should get me a good job with so many translators and interpreters of German needed, but I may have to do military service. I was allowed to finish my studies because the war was ending, but they're still conscripting people. If I've to do three or four years it wouldn't be fair to ask Alice to wait even if she's interested."

"You two are discussing my future, so I think I've a right to say something," Alice told them as she re-filled George's cup. "I want you, George, now or at any other time, and the sooner the better. Even if you don't manage to get a good job I have money of my own and can earn more. I'd want you even if you were out on the roads with a brush and shovel. If you're called to the forces it will make no difference. Rich or poor, I belong to you. I did before, so don't think I only say this because you rescued me. The only difference that makes is now I want you to know it. I think we should make plans very soon, army or not."

Just then her father came into the room. "Are you alright, Alice?"

"Yes, I'm less upset now, but I was frightened. I would offer you a cup of tea, but I've given your ration to George."

"So long after hostilities and tea still rationed," Walter said in disgust. "Well, if George got it he earned it. Alice poured her father a cup of tea, and he smiled when he saw that she could tease after her ordeal. "George, you don't know how relieved I was when I saw you were there and that fiend was bleeding. I'll be in your debt for ever."

"You don't need to be, Dad, I want to marry him as soon as possible. When you give me away you'll have settled your debt."

"Oh, has he taken advantage of the situation and proposed whilst you were grateful?"

"No, Walter, you wrong him," his wife told him. "Alice has declared herself. George and I were talking, and she said her piece. George is innocent, but now he'll be thinking about the future a little more urgently."

"Yes, I'll have to save up for a wheelbarrow and a brush," he said with a very serious look on his face. "The trouble is there are so many unknowns. Will I have to go into the forces? Will I get a decent job?"

"As I see it," Walter began, "it's time for another conference. We can't think for the Government, but now we are all sure of the wishes of both of you we must try to make your dreams come true. I'll say that I'm pleased you've now put the pot on to boil, until you both made the decision public we were unable to help you. Now we may be. Will you arrange a day for your parents to come again, George? I know that you're fully of age now, but I think it only courteous to include your family in any discussion of your future."

"I'll try. Is there any day unsuitable for you?"

"None that I know of, if you fix the date we'll do the rest. Now, wife of mine, we must let these two happy people have a while alone. They've a lot to say to each other. This hasn't been too bad a day after all."

He led his wife from the room and Alice threw herself into George's arms. "You don't know how long I've wanted this," she said as she kissed him. George wasn't slow to join in her pleasure.

+ + +

Gwen Briggs looked up from the table when she heard footsteps outside. It was a warm sunny morning, and although she had the door open she was very hot. There was a good fire burning, part of which had been pushed under the oven. On the table were pastry and a bowl of meat and vegetables. She left the baking and went to the door to meet the village constable from Cottley. He leaned his bicycle against the railings of the tiny garden.

"Good morning, Constable," Gwen greeted him. "We don't often get a visit from you."

"No, Mrs Briggs. Is your son George at home?"

"Yes, he's upstairs. Come in and I'll call him. Is something wrong?"

The officer entered the room and sat on a chair near the door. "You will hear when George comes."

Gwen called upstairs and her son entered the room a few minutes later.

"Good morning, what can I do for you?" he enquired of the visitor.

"You can take this summons off my hands. You're required to attend the Magistrates' Court on Monday morning at 10.30. What have you been up to lad?"

"Is this about Wilfred Baker?" George wondered as he took the document.

"Yes, it seems that you have been a bit rough with him, and he doesn't like it."

"He won't," Gwen remarked. "Bullies never do when their turn comes to be punished. Would you like a cup of tea after your journey?"

"Yes please, Mrs. Briggs. Its thirsty work pedalling a bicycle today, and I see that you've another warm job."

"It certainly is when you have to light a fire for the oven on a nice day like this. In summer I hate baking."

Gwen had prepared the pie whilst they were talking and now she put it in the oven and adjusted the damper, an iron plate that slotted into the flu to control the temperature. She then filled the kettle and put it on the front of the fire.

"It'll not be long," she said as she prepared the teapot and produced cups and saucers.

"When you've drunk your tea will you come with me to visit Miss Shepherd at the mill house? George asked the policeman.

"I've to pass there, so if you can show me a good reason I'll do so."

"I want you to see and hear why I have received this summons. Your responsibility ended when you gave it to me, but you need to know what kind of people live in the area you look after. Alice can both tell and show you."

Gwen poured the tea and gave the visitor a piece of cake. "That's the end of last week's baking. We seem to have it measured pretty well considering the small rations we still get. George was away until yesterday, so we didn't get his last week."

The student and the policeman walked together to the Shepherd home, the officer pushed his bike. George knocked on the door, and it was opened by Alice.

"Hello," she greeted George, "is there something wrong?" she added as she saw who his companion was.

"Yes, I want him to talk with you and see that dress."

"You must come in then," and she stepped back and held the door open for them.

Mrs Shepherd came through an inner door as they entered.

"What's wrong, George?" she asked.

"My prophecy has been fulfilled. Our friend here has brought me a summons to attend the Magistrates' Court on Monday. I'm accused of assault and battery on Wilfred Baker. I said we'd hear more about it."

"Yes, and it's probably all lies. Alice, show the policeman your dress, then he'll know the sort of fiend we have in the valley."

"You were expecting trouble for Mr. Briggs?"

"We know Jean Baker. She believes that her son is an angel, but we all have known different for many years."

Alice returned with the torn dress and showed it to the constable. "This is what Jean Baker's angel did whilst I was wearing it. I can't show you the bruise he gave me at the same time, but the location of the tear will give you some idea of where it is. If George hadn't arrived he'd have raped me."

"The officer turned to George, "I see now why you wanted me to come here. Of course I can do nothing in this case, but it's as well for me to know such people. I'll give you some good advice, assault and battery is a very serious charge, but as Miss Shepherd tells it you had good reason. You should see a lawyer and get him to help you with your defence. It sounds as if Baker is the one who should be in Court."

"That's true, and we did think of reporting it, but it only happened yesterday afternoon," Mrs. Shepherd told him. "My husband was going to phone his lawyer today, partly to protect George."

"Tell him to do that. Have you a lawyer, Mr. Briggs?"

"I've never had need of one, and after Dad was unemployed so long I can't afford one."

"No, but we can," Alice told him. "I'll phone Dad and ask him to come up."

Alice used the house extension and ten minutes later her father came into the room.

"Hello Constable. What's happening?"

"I got a summons to go to court on a charge of assault and battery. I asked the officer to come here to see what sort of character we have in the area. He may attack some other poor girl when there's no protector around. Now he's given me some good advice."

"I've seen the dress, and I think Mr. Briggs should have a lawyer with him on Monday, otherwise things could go wrong. This is a very serious matter."

"I was going to ring my solicitor. I'll do it now and ask him to defend George and I'll pay his fee. Don't worry about that, George."

"Now that's settled it's time for me to get moving," the policeman said. "I wish you good luck on Monday, Mr. Briggs."

"Thank you for the advice," George said as he watched him mount his bike.

Walter went to the phone, returning a few minutes later to find that the lovers had moved into the lounge for a short time.

"George, are you free to go to the lawyer's office this afternoon for 3.30? I'll take you and Alice in the car with the dress."

"Yes, I've no other commitment."

"Right, be here for 2.30."

George went home in time to see his mother take the pie from the oven and put other items in it. She pushed more wood under and reset the damper, then cut two large pieces from the pie for their lunch.

"Mr. Shepherd will take me and Alice to see his solicitor this afternoon. Bobby Clarke advised me to have one to lead my defence."

"Can you afford it?"

"Alice's dad will cover any cost, he's promised."

After lunch George prepared for the journey, and when the time came he walked up to the mill house with the summons. When the trio entered the lawyers office Walter was greeted as a long-standing and valued client.

"This is George Briggs. Give him the summons, George."

For a few minutes nothing was said, then the lawyer laid the paper on his desk.

"Now, Mr. Briggs, tell me what you did to get this summons."

"I stopped a brute from attacking and raping my fiancé. She wasn't officially my fiancé at the time, but she is now. We were expecting something like this as we know him and his mother, and I did make a mess of his face."

"Did you use a lot of force?"

"All that I could. He was always vicious in our school days, not just to my brother and me, but to any child smaller than he was. Mr. Pighills threatened to kick him out of the school at one stage. Now he's grown to be a big man, and for the last seven years the army's been training him how to be more efficient at hurting and killing. I had to overcome him quickly whilst his hands were occupied or Alice and I would both have suffered."

"Perhaps you should tell me the whole story as it happened."

George did so and mentioned the torn dress. "Have you still got it?" asked the lawyer whose name was Mr. Selman.

"It's here," Alice said as she held it out for him to see.

He examined the tear and noted its position. "Bring it to the court on Monday. Will you be going?" he asked Walter.

"You bet I will, and my son too. I also wondered about getting Charles Pighills to come. He's retired now, so will probably be free. He can testify to George's good nature and Baker's brutality."

"Do you think you can get him?"

"Yes, he's a friend of mine."

"Then I see no reason to worry, Mr. Briggs. Of course you can never tell with magistrates, but I'll try to get Baker charged with attempted rape. He turned to Alice, "Did he say that he was going to rape you?"

"He suggested that George and I did other things beside bird watching. He said that he was going to have some of what George was getting."

"That sounds near enough. Whatever you do make sure that you aren't late. Try to be there half an hour beforehand. I'll be there by 9.45, but we may have to hang around all morning if there are other cases before us."

"When they got home Walter telephoned Mr. Pighills who was very willing to show up to give character references, both good and bad, for his former pupils.

On Friday it was payday at the mill and both the Bakers found that they had an extra week's money in lieu of notice.

"What is this?" Jean demanded.

"You are both fired. Not only did your son attempt to rape my daughter, but her rescuer has to appear in court accused of assault and battery. As you know that is a serious charge that would ruin his career if he were found guilty. No relative of Wilfred Baker will ever enter my property again."

"Even if this had been true, and I know it isn't, we wouldn't be to blame," Joe said.

"We've had trouble with your son and your wife before. Had your wife not supported him in his evil ways since childhood he'd know now that it doesn't pay. You're equally guilty in that you allowed her to encourage his cruelty by always protecting him. I want you both off my property for ever."

Jean immediately tried to get the other workers to join in a protest against the dismissals. Walter called every employee to a meeting in the last half hour of the working day.

"Ladies and gentlemen," he began, "I call you that because normally we have a good relationship in this mill. Jean and Joe Baker have been dismissed for a very good reason, as I believe you will agree when you hear the facts. Jean wants you all to strike to get them reinstated. It won't happen, so I'll tell you why before you take an action that you'd regret.

"On Wednesday their son Wilfred, attempted to rape my daughter Alice, whom you all know. He tore her dress and badly bruised her. George Briggs arrived on the scene by chance, and was able to stop him before he achieved his foul intentions. Now George has to go to court to answer a charge of assault and battery because he hurt the darling boy. Because he protected her they're now trying to ruin the career he's worked so hard to obtain. If you had a daughter, and I know some of you have, and she suffered an attack like that, would you want his parents on your payroll?"

A chorus of 'No' thundered out, which wasn't surprising as most of the employees were women.

On Monday morning George rode with Walter, his son and daughter to the courthouse. There they met Mr. Selman, a tall man aged about forty-five, with dark hair and wearing a charcoal grey suit.

"Now, let me advise you, Mr. Briggs," he said. "Unless asked about the earlier trouble with Baker and his mother don't mention it. Tell only what you are asked by the clerk of the court or anyone else, including me. Mr. Pighills is here, and he'll tell of the bullying of you and other children. It will be better coming from him.

"Similarly, Miss Shepherd, if you are asked if he bullied you it would be wise just to point out that your father was his parents' employer. It would have been foolish of him if he picked on you.

"Mr. Ernest, unless you are asked don't mention pulling George off Baker, we don't want them saying that he'd lost control of himself.

"Don't worry, Mr. Briggs, you may be bound over to keep the peace, but even that's unlikely. Now it's 10.15 so we ought to go in."

George was separated from the others and placed in the dock. Mrs. Baker and her son were sitting together. As it came near to the time for the court to start those not immediately wanted were asked to leave the room. They were fortunate in that their case was the first on the list. All those remaining had to stand whilst the magistrates entered and took their seats. George was pleased to see that one of them was a woman, no woman would be sympathetic to a rapist.

The Clerk of the court opened the case against George. Mr. Selman told the court that he would be representing George and there was another lawyer conducting the case for the prosecution. Wilfred was put in the witness box where he took the oath and gave his name and address.

"Please tell the court what happened near Harker's Mill on Wednesday last." the prosecutor requested.

"I went for a walk and was on the path near the dam when I saw Miss Shepherd enter a small hide near the water. I hadn't seen her for years as I have been away fighting Germans in North Africa, Italy and other places. We were at school together, so I left the path and went to speak with her."

"Then what happened?"

"She told me I was trespassing, so I said that I just wanted to speak to her after being away all those years. The next thing I knew Briggs rushed in and hit me in the face several times, bursting my nose and cutting my eyebrow."

"Did he cause those scars on your face?"

"Yes, then he threw me against a wooden post and nearly knocked me out."

"Can you explain why he acted in this way?"

"No, he probably was jealous because I was speaking with Miss Shepherd."

A doctor was then called who gave evidence about the damage to the face. Mr. Selman didn't challenge any of the evidence so far. Now George's defence began and his lawyer stood up after the oath was taken.

"Mr. Briggs, you've heard the account given by Mr. Baker about what happened. Is it true?"

"No, sir, it's a pack of lies."

"Then please tell us why you were there, and why you went into the hide."

"For a long time I've had Mr. Shepherd's permission to go on his land to watch the wild life, mainly birds. I built the hide for Miss Shepherd and myself to watch without disturbing them. On Wednesday I came home from University for the Easter break. Miss Shepherd had written to me, telling me about a pair of great crested grebes that seemed to be about to breed on the dam. I'd been travelling a long time, all the way from Cambridge, so after some refreshment at home I decided to walk along to the hide and get some fresh air and try to see the birds."

"Did you expect to see Mr. Baker there?"

"No."

"Did you expect to see Miss Shepherd there?"

"I thought it possible, she's almost as keen a bird watcher as I am."

"When did you learn that Mr. Baker was there?"

"As I approached I heard Miss Shepherd scream, then cry out, 'Get off me, you brute. Help me someone.'"

"What did you do when you heard that?"

"I rushed in to do as she asked."

"What did you find?"

"Baker had Miss Shepherd in a corner. He had one arm around behind her head and his other hand was gripping her breast. Her dress was ripped and he was trying to force her to kiss him."

"So what did you do?"

"I hit him until he let her go."

"Thank you, Mr. Briggs."

The Baker lawyer then stood up to cross examine. "How long have you known Mr. Baker?"

"Ever since we were at school."

"During those years have you hit him before?"

"No, on the contrary he used to hit both myself and my younger brother, he's older than us and liked to hurt us."

"Was that why you were so savage on Wednesday? I suggest that it was an old grudge and nothing to do with Miss Shepherd."

"That is not true. I knew from the past that he's a bully, now he's had seven years in the army being trained how to be even more vicious. All the training that I have ever had was a few bouts in the boxing ring at the Grammar School. I knew that unless I got in first before he could get his hands off his victim neither of us would have a chance. I didn't know then that Mr. Shepherd Junior was fairly close behind me. I had to get a quick advantage."

The lawyer saw that such evidence was not helping his case so he sat down. Alice was the next witness.

"What is your relationship with these two men?" Mr. Selman asked.

"I've never had any kind of relationship with Mr. Baker. Mr. Briggs has been my friend for about ten years and we hope to marry in the near future."

"Please tell the court what happened when Mr. Baker arrived."

"I told him it was private land and he must go away. I didn't want him to frighten the birds. He then said that he knew it was private land, but that Mr. Briggs was allowed to come there. He suggested that we did other things beside watching birds, and with a lot of foul language he said that he wanted some of what Briggs was getting. His accusations were untrue, I am a virgin.

"He then threw one arm behind my head and grabbed my left breast so savagely that my dress was ripped beyond repair, and he bruised me badly, still saying what was to come next. I screamed as loudly as I could and George rushed in and stopped him."

The dress was shown to the court and the magistrates examined it carefully, the woman in particular was really thorough as she held it.

The Baker lawyer tried to shake Alice's story until she cried out, "Why do you keep repeating the same questions? Do you want a rapist to get away with what he did and ruin the life of a good man?"

The chief magistrate drew her attention to the fact that it was George who was on trial, not Baker, but he told the lawyer that there was no need for further harassment.

Ernest then took the oath and Mr. Selman asked, "Why did you go to the hide?"

"My father and I heard her scream in the mill. I'd to go down two flights of old steps and run up to the hide. Fortunately George was much nearer."

"What did you find when you got there?"

"My sister was cowering in a corner, trying to hold her torn dress and cover her decency. George had just hit Baker and knocked him off balance. He hit the side of his head on one of the wooden supports of the hide and seemed to be half stunned."

"Was Mr. Briggs still hitting him after he hit his head on the post?"

"No, there was no need. My father followed me in, and when he knew the circumstances he sent Baker away quickly."

The other lawyer stood up. "Mr. Shepherd, you were inside a working textile mill, yet you claim that you heard the alleged scream. Can you explain how that could be?"

"Easily, sir. The hide is only about twenty yards from the water wheel. It was a very hot day, and all the windows were wide open. We scarcely notice the sound of the machines, but when my sister screamed as loud as she could not only my father and I but several of the hands heard it."

Finally Mr. Pighills was called and gave his name and address. "What is your occupation?" Mr. Selman asked

"I am a retired headmaster."

"Where did you teach?"

"At Cullerton school, for twenty years."

"Do you know Mr. Baker and Mr. Briggs?"

"Very well."

"Please tell the court what you know of their characters during their school days."

"Mr Briggs was always a quiet and studious boy and I was glad when I knew he had passed a scholarship for the Grammar School. The other, Mr. Baker, was a vicious bully, always trying to hurt those smaller than himself."

"Thank you, Mr. Pighills. That completes our case for the defence, Your Honours. You will have seen that Mr. Briggs should never have been in the dock. As a peaceful citizen who had to use violence to protect an innocent young lady he should be honoured, not persecuted. Mr. Wilfred Baker should be where he is, accused of attempted rape."

The three magistrates conferred, but it didn't take long. The chief of them gave their decision, "Mr Briggs, you are found 'Not Guilty' of the charge. We understand that it was your fiancé whom you were defending, but that makes no difference. You are free to go."

"Mr Wilfred Baker, we are very disturbed by this case and intend to pass a copy of the court record to the police with a recommendation that you be arrested and charged with attempted rape."

"We knew it would all be fixed, like it was before," yelled Jean Baker. "Wilfred is a good man, but they've always ganged up against him. The Shepherds and the Pighills always stick up for the Briggs lot."

"Be quiet, woman. This is a court of law, not Bradford Market."

"Why can't I say a good word for my boy? You let the other lot lie for Briggs."

"Another word from you, woman, and I will sentence you for contempt of court. The case is over."

"Yes, and a farce it is. Instead of punishing him for what he did to a man who has been fighting for his country you try to say that my boy is a rapist."

"Officer, take her down. Woman, you will serve four weeks from today at one of His Majesty's prisons for contempt of court. Let it be a lesson for you."

CHAPTER 10

When Jean Hudson was released from prison she was both bitter and angry. Joe was at home when she got there.

"Hello, Jean. How are you after being in that awful place?"

"I'm alright, but it's a rotten system when a mother can't speak her mind when her son is mistreated."

"A court of law isn't the right place. In any case Wilfred is a very lucky man. The police and prosecutor's office wanted to arrest him, but the people you love to malign pleaded with them to let the matter drop."

"Only because they knew that he didn't do it. My son isn't a rapist."

"That's your problem, Jean. You think that he's a saint, but all these people can't be wrong. The Briggs boys, each on a separate occasion, Nora Donovan, Doris Slater, Mr. Pighills and the Shepherds all have accused him of a variety of vicious things and it's now become a serious matter."

"They're all in it together."

"You're blind to his faults, and you've cost us our jobs. He's not as nice and good as you think. You never accepted he needed punishment, and now we've a monster on our hands."

"You're talking daft as usual. What are all these boxes doing here?"

"We're moving to Burnston. I've got a job at Brown and Smith's weaving shed and there's one for you as well."

"I don't want to leave here. I won't let that lot drive me out of Harker's Bridge."

"They're not driving you out. We're going to where we can get work. Thanks to your darling son we've none here and won't get any. I'm going to take the furniture I need to a cottage there, you can please yourself whether you come or not."

"You can't just move without me having a look at the house."

"You've had too much say in things. From now on I'll do as Walter Shepherd said when you were a fool over George Briggs' Scholarship. I'll make the decisions from now on. If you don't want to accept that you can stay here, but you'll have to tell the landlord, because I put in our notice last Friday."

"Jean looked aghast when she heard her husband's declared intentions.

"I'm your wife, you can't do this."

"Can't I? We'll see. I'm going to walk across to the cottage now to get it ready for moving in. You can come with me or stay, it's your choice."

Jean had made herself a cup of tea when they were arguing, so she drank it and put on again the coat that she'd come home in.

"I'll come, but if I don't like it I'm not moving. We don't know anybody there. What about Wilfred?"

"He has a job at the quarry, so he'll be nearer there than here. If he causes any more trouble he's out. I'm fed up with his ways."

"You wouldn't kick your own son out of his home surely?"

"Oh yes, if he causes me any more trouble."

"If he goes I go."

"That's your choice. Now if you're coming we must set off. We need to be there before the fish and chip shop shuts or we'll get no dinner."

122

Their journey through the woods wasn't the happy and peaceful one that it should have been. As they walked by the gurgling stream they didn't hear it, or the singing of the birds in the trees. Jean was surly and grumbled as she walked. As they climbed the hill into Burston village she looked about her.

"Where is this house?"

"Just by the mill. We'll be there in a couple of minutes." They walked past the mill. "There it is, the end one of the row."

Jean looked and as they got nearer she took notice of everything about her. Whilst Joe unlocked the door she peered in through the window, and then followed him into the cottage. She opened the cupboard doors, looked in the pantry and climbed the stairs to see both the bedrooms.

"You'll have noticed that we've electricity here as well as gas for cooking, hot and cold water, and a water closet instead of the tub down the yard. We'll be much better off."

"It'll do, I suppose, but it's not right for a man to decide all this when his wife isn't there."

"If you hadn't been a fool you'd have been there."

"How are you going to get the furniture here?"

"Harry Turner will move it on his lorry on Saturday."

Saturday came and the move was made. Wilfred was working during the morning when the lorry was loaded, but he arrived at the new home just about the same time as the furniture. Grudgingly he obeyed his father's order to help carry it indoors. By five o'clock the beds were in place and Jean began to fix up the curtains that happened to be the right size for the windows.

"We'll be able to get some new tools now. We need one of those new washing machines, an electric kettle, a toaster and an electric iron to start with."

"Yes, eventually. We've been out of work for seven weeks and I'd to pay two rents this week, one on each house. I paid Harry £2/10/- for moving us.

You'll not buy anything, electric or otherwise, apart from food and cleaning materials, until we've an adequate reserve, about £30."

When Constance learned that her only friend was leaving the valley she was horrified. "What am I going to do, Jean? I've no other friends here, and I'm barred from the dances for speaking the truth."

"Think yourself lucky, I got four weeks in prison for the same thing."

When the Bakers had gone Constance was distraught. She saw all her neighbours happily living and chatting together. Helen and Richard were usually out all day at the small office they had rented, but she saw them at weekends with the Briggs and Donovan families. Doris and her mother were also glad to be part of the friendly group.

Winter arrived and she was even lonelier. She'd no visitors except for her brothers who occasionally came to check on her welfare, but their visits were always brief. She'd begun to go further afield, and although Cottley was over a mile away she began to go there at weekends. Sometimes she went to the King's Head at Cullerton as well. There was a heavy fall of snow and it lingered for a full week. Then it began to thaw, but when only half of it had melted there was a sharp frost. On top of the ice that had formed another few inches of snow settled.

During this period of treacherous lanes and dark nights Constance limited her outings to daylight hours. On one occasion she had enjoyed the company at the Dog and Gun in Cottley so much that she stayed until the three o'clock closing time. As she left the building she noticed that fog was developing and it was almost dark. She began to walk home, and as she did so she thought of the time when she could go to the Hilltop, only half a mile from home. It was thawing again, and the softness of the snow on the ice made some parts very difficult.

+ + +

"I think that we'll stop work now. It's a suitable place for me to stop, and I don't like the look of the weather," Richard said. Quickly Helen covered her typewriter and put the papers that she'd been working with into a folder before putting on her outer garments. Richard locked the office door and they went out to the car.

124

"We'll miss calling at the pub today," he said. "This fog is bad and getting worse. With all the ice under the snow I'll have to drive very slowly."

Carefully he manoeuvred the car along the narrow twisting lane. He turned into the other short lane that dropped down the slope into Harker's Bridge.

"What's that?" Helen asked, "It looks like a body."

"It's Constance," Richard said after he had stopped the car and got out. "She's unconscious by the look of her."

They hurried to her side and found he had been right. Close to her head was a large stone sticking up out of the snow. On it was blood and they saw a wound on her forehead.

"She's slipped and hit her head on that stone," Richard said. "You stay here and I'll go to the mill house to phone for a doctor or an ambulance. Get the rugs out of the car and cover her."

Walter rang for the ambulance, and by the time that Richard was back with his wife it was coming down the lane followed by a police car. The crew examined the patient and loaded her into their vehicle. Richard took his car forward so that the others could turn at the junction by the mill house. The ambulance left immediately and the police searched the area with powerful torches for evidence of what had happened. They then began to question the Mouldings.

After getting the names of the witnesses the officer asked, "Do you know the lady?"

"Yes, she's Miss Constance Manning who lives next door to us."

"What do you know about her lying there unconscious?"

"No more than you do. We were coming home and my wife saw her lying there. I hadn't seen her; I was too busy fighting the fog and ice."

"What did you do?"

"We got out of the car, and when we saw that she was injured I went to the mill house to get help whilst my wife covered her with our car rugs."

"Was she awake? Did she speak?"

"No."

After the police had left the author took his wife home and she began to prepare the evening meal.

"I hope that she'll be alright," Helen said. "If she was there long she could have hyperthermia."

"It's most unlikely that she'd be concerned if she'd found you."

"That's true, but I'm not vindictive. She's a woman and our neighbour. I'll telephone the hospital when we get to the office tomorrow to find out how she is."

When she enquired she learned that Constance was awake, but would have to stay in the hospital at least two days as she was slightly concussed. She also learned that there was a visiting time that evening between seven and eight o'clock.

"I'll go to see her," she told Richard. "She lives alone and someone should see that she has what she needs. She has brothers, but I don't know how to contact them."

"I'll take you after we eat," Richard promised, "but don't be surprised if she refuses to see you."

When they arrived at the hospital they were directed to a ward where they found Constance sitting up in bed with a dressing on her head.

"Why have you come?" she asked in surprise. "You're the last people I expected to see."

"We're here because we wanted to know how you are," Helen told her.

"Why are you concerned? You aren't my friends."

"I wanted to be, but you didn't. That doesn't matter now. How are you?"

"I'll live. Who sent me here?"

"We found you and sent for the ambulance."

"You found me?"

"Yes, you were lying unconscious in the snow. There was a large stone near your head with blood on it. You must have fallen on it."

"So that's why my head aches. I must thank you. Fancy it being you of all people. You may have saved my life, but I think it might have been better if you'd left me there."

"Don't say that, you're a young woman with all of your life before you."

The nurse came to take her temperature whilst they were there, and Richard gave her his telephone number. "When she's ready to come home give me a ring in working hours and I'll fetch her," he said.

"There's no need for that," Constance protested, "I can get a taxi."

"We'll come, and we'll get you home. I know that for some reason you do not like Helen, but as your nearest neighbours it's our duty to help you."

Two days later the call came in the morning. The doctor had just seen Constance, and she was considered fit to return home. They finished what they were doing and went out to the car. Since their marriage Richard had traded in the two-seater for a Morris that would hold four, or a reasonable amount of shopping when needed.

"I'm glad I changed cars," he said. "I couldn't have fetched her in the two-seater."

"Why, do you think that she'd have led you astray?"

"From her past record she might have tried."

"Why did you insist on doing this?"

"We are next door neighbours, Jean has left and she's lonely, so it's a good time to try to bury the hatchet. If there's any decency in her at all she can't hate us after we saved her from a night in the snow, maybe from death. If she's any sense she'll apologise for what she said in the bar. Nigel will probably lift his ban, she'll be able to go to the pub and the dances, and we'll have peace in Harker's Bridge."

"I hope it'll work," Helen said. "I never wanted that ill feeling and all the nastiness. There was never any sense in it."

When they arrived at the hospital Constance was waiting in the foyer. Richard got out of the car, opened the rear door and saw her settled with a rug over her legs.

"You must have saved my life, and now you're going out of your way to get me home. Helen, I've hated you, but I can't hate someone who's doing all this for me. I feel really bad about this," she said as the car began to move.

"So far as I'm concerned that's all in the past. I never knew why you disliked me, so far as I'm aware I never did anything to earn it. We live in a peaceful valley and we shouldn't spoil it with bad relationships."

"Yes, I feel very sorry about it. I suppose I got jealous because you had so many friends here and I only had Jean. She said a lot of things about the Briggs boys and you're friendly with them. With one thing and another I began to really hate you, but I see now that I was the one in the wrong. Apart from this help that you are giving me, will you forgive me and allow me to be your friend from now on?"

"Of course. I want for nothing more than peace between us, that's how it should be. Let's never mention the past again."

"Thank you. I never expected you to forgive me after the things I've said, especially that day in the bar when Nigel barred me. I see now that he did the right thing. It was your special day and I tried to spoil it."

"We'll try to get him to let you come back now. You must have missed the dances."

"Yes, I did."

"We'll call in tomorrow and tell him and ask him to let you return," Richard promised. "Have you enough to eat in the house?"

"I would like to call in a shop, but I've almost no money with me. If I'd used a taxi he'd have had to wait until I got some from the house to pay him."

"What do you need?" I can lend you some money."

"In that case will you lend me five shillings? That will do me fine until I'm fit to go to the village."

They stopped at a corner shop and Richard took a ten shilling note out of his wallet. Helen went into the shop with her to make sure that she was alright.

"Thank you again," Constance said. "I just can't believe that it's all happened like this."

"Well just enjoy being friendly with your neighbour," Richard told her.

"I can't understand it either," Helen told her husband when they were alone. "If it lasts I'll not need to, all I'll have to do is enjoy the peace."

"We must hope it will last," Richard agreed. "Peace has come to Harker's Bridge, long may it reign."

CHAPTER 11

George Briggs had been home just over six weeks after finishing his education at Cambridge. He wasn't sure what would happen next, but he hoped there wouldn't be too long a delay before he found out. Until he was sure what his near future would be there was no point in trying to find employment compatible with his qualifications. He received an envelope with official lettering on it in the Tuesday post. After he'd read the contents he passed it to his mother.

"It's come. I've to report to a Government office in Leeds next Monday at eleven o'clock. There'll be a medical and an interview."

"It looks as if they want you for the forces. At least the war is over, but that means they'll have both of you unless you fail the medical. Your father did, but it was his eyesight and I don't think you have any problem there."

"Our Alec doesn't seem to be too unhappy, and as you say the fighting has stopped. Once the initial training is finished it may not be too bad."

A similar conversation took place that evening when he went to the mill house and took Alice to the hide.

"You may not have to go into the armed forces, but a medical doesn't sound too good. We'll have to hope for the best," Alice told him. "If you do have to go I'll miss you."

"I'll write every week if I can, and it may be possible to telephone. We can plan nothing until we know, so let's enjoy this evening and watch that kingfisher try to get his supper."

When Monday came Alice borrowed her father's car and took her lover to Leeds. They parked the car and found the office where George had to report. Alice then went to look around the shops. As they had no idea how long it would take for George to have the examination and interview they agreed Alice would visit the car every hour. George would meet her there whenever he was free.

George then went into the building and gave his name to a soldier on duty at the door. A few minutes later he was taken into a room where a thorough medical examination took place. From there he had to go to another room where two men were seated at a table. They were both middle aged and wore civilian clothes. One was clean-shaven and had a full head of grey hair and a pale countenance as if he rarely saw the sun. This man addressed George and told him to sit in the chair facing them both.

"Mr. Briggs, you've been given time to complete your education at Cambridge University. The war is over, but there's still a need for many young people to put the continent of Europe back into a safe condition. How do you feel about this?"

"I'm thankful I was allowed to complete the courses and obtain the qualifications I strived for. I more or less expected I would be called on to give some period now that has been accomplished. I won't rejoice, but realise there's nothing I can do about it."

"You have been studying the German language, I think."

"Both German and French, sir."

"How well did you do in your finals?"

"As well as possible in both languages."

"Yes, so I see from the University's report. Mr Stead will now ask you some questions."

Mr. Stead was a tall man with a short black beard and spectacles with thick lenses. He wore a dark grey suit and a red tie. He addressed George in German. He asked several questions and was answered in the same language. He then switched without warning to French and again George replied in the same tongue. The two men then conferred after sending George to another room for a cup of tea.

When he had left the room Mr Stead turned to his companion. "I think that we've found a special one here. His accent in both languages is exceptional and his replies were quick and comprehensive. This man mustn't be wasted in the armed forces. He's one of those we were told to watch out for, and he's at the top end of them."

"Good, he seems to be a sensible sort, and he has to be intelligent to have such honours from the university. We'll send him to London and let them find a job for him. Is he really that good?"

"I had a surprise when I heard his German. His accent is perfect, and the French is nearly as good. He's exceptional for an Englishman. German isn't the easiest language to learn to speak."

When George was called into the room again the first interviewer addressed him. "Mr. Stead tells me your German is of a very high quality. We have been asked to look out for those who speak the language, and your French will be useful as well. We'll now arrange for you to go to London to meet higher officials. You'll be sent details and a travel pass will be included with the order. Remember that although this won't be military the instructions will be equally enforced by law. Now you may go home and do what you wish until you hear from us, probably next week."

George left the building and made his way to the car. The time was five minutes to one, so he arrived just before Alice made her hourly check.

"How did it go, dear?"

"I'm not sure. The medical examiner said I'm very healthy, and then I met two men in civilian clothes. One of them questioned me in both German and French, and then I was sent to get a cup of tea whilst they conferred. When I came back I was ordered to go to London to see someone else. It seems that I may be in line for a non-military post where my linguistic abilities can be used."

"That sounds good, apart from the fact that you'll be away from Harker's Bridge. If its civilian you will be safer than if it had to be military."

"He said that the London interview wouldn't be military, so I'm hoping that they'll find me something in administration or logistics. There'll be supply lines for the German people, repairs to the transport system, hospitals and other things, plus the trials of war criminals. As I also speak French I could be used to help with matters that are handled internationally."

"It sounds better than being shot at. Now we must find some food before we go home."

A few days later the postman brought another official letter. It ordered him to go to a certain address in the centre of London and show the document to the person on duty at the door. Enclosed was a travel voucher for a two-way journey to King's Cross. The order was for him to go two days after the letter arrived.

George took the letter to the mill house after his mother had seen it. All the family were at lunch when he arrived.

"George, I think that you're a lucky fellow," Ernest told him. "I never got anything like this. All I got was an order to go to an army camp. It looks as though you'll drop into a special job. Don't build up your hopes too much, but to me it looks good."

"I agree," Walter said. "They don't usually send people to London on free passes when they want them in the forces."

"George is special," Alice pointed out. "They've realised this and want him in a special job."

"Then it's a pity that it isn't in Cullerton," George commented.

+ + +

When he walked out of King's Cross Station George stood in awe. He'd moved from the quietness of Harker's Bridge and the village to the town in order to attend the Grammar School. At Cambridge he encountered even more traffic when he ventured off campus. None of that prepared him for the wide road and the many vehicles passing the station. He noticed a taxi rank, and realised that if he hoped to get to his appointment on time he'd have to use one of the cars he saw there. To arrive late would be a serious crime in the eyes of officialdom.

So far he'd used none of the money he'd brought with him but now he bought a drink and a sandwich. Once his physical needs were satisfied he approached the first car in the rank. The driver was a middle aged woman with a motherly face. He showed her the letter, and asked if she could get him there on time.

"Yes, dear, I'll take you there. Is this your first time in London?"

"It is. That's why I'm taking a taxi. I mustn't be late, and I've no idea how to get there myself."

He found there was a considerable distance to go and was glad that he hadn't tried to find his own way. The driver pointed out to him various sights of interest and told him things about places they passed. When he had paid her at his destination she gave him some good advice.

"You can get to King's Cross either by bus or train, and it will be much cheaper than taxi. Ask someone at the place where you're going or a policeman. Don't tell anyone else that you're new to the city. There are crooks who watch for people like you to prey on them."

"Thank you," he said with gratitude before he entered the building and showed his order to the man at the door. He passed George on to a lady who took him to a room where he waited a few minutes whilst she took the order through an inner door. She then returned, and showed him into the second room.

A tall gentleman with a bald head and gold rimmed spectacles was seated at a very large desk. He was wearing a dark blue suit. Beside him was another man with a broad head of iron grey hair cropped short, and he wore a grey suit and tie.

"Come in and sit down, Mr. Briggs," the man at the desk ordered. "I am Sir Alfred Hawkins, and I'm in charge of finding suitable people to do special things in the conquered countries. In this case we want you for the territory of Germany controlled by the Western Allies. My companion is Herr Heinrich Wagner who is helping me with specialist advice.

"We aren't military in any way, but so far as you are concerned my authority and powers are equal to those of a high ranking army officer. What I order will not normally be countermanded by anyone but an undertaker."

George heard all of this with mixed thoughts, it seemed that he could be entering a situation that could be as threatening as a military one.

"Good morning, Herr Briggs," the other man greeted him in his own tongue. "We've been told you have some knowledge of my language. When you speak to me I don't want to hear one word of English. I want to find out if it is true what they say about you."

For over half an hour Herr Wagner shot questions and comments at George who replied briskly and with confidence. After they spoke on several subjects the German turned to Sir Alfred and spoke to him in English.

"This man is good. I have only known three English who had equal ability, and I've met many." He turned to George and asked in English," Who taught you German? Did you have knowledge of it other than what you learned at school and Cambridge?"

"No, sir, but one or my tutors was a German, a Herr Gustav Strauss."

George was taken from the room by a secretary and led to a canteen.

"Get some food and wait here until I fetch you," she ordered.

George went to the counter and asked the lady behind it for a cup of tea.

"Do you wish for any food?" she asked.

"Could you tell me the prices please? My money is limited, and I still have a long journey home."

"Eat what you like, sir, there are no charges. Whilst you're here you are under the authority of Sir Alfred, and he's ordered that you don't starve."

On hearing this George ordered a bowl of soup and a roll. He would have liked more, but he didn't know how soon the secretary would return for him. He'd just finished eating when she arrived and took him back to the two men.

"Please sit down, Mr. Briggs," Sir Alfred requested in a less commanding manner than before. "We've discussed your future and before making final decisions I want to ask you some personal questions. Are you married?"

"No, but I'm engaged and waiting to see what my immediate future will be."

"It can be very good, I would say, but if you take up my offer you'll have to wait a little while for the wedding. Who is your next of kin?"

"Both of my parents, William and Gwendoline Briggs."

"What, if any, is your religion?"

"Christian."

"Roman Catholic, Anglican or other?"

"I used to go to a Methodist chapel before going to university. Now I'm attending there again, but I'm not fully committed to their doctrines on some matters."

"You have not done service because you were studying both German and French. Now you must use them for the good of all our countries or go into the army. I would advise you to think carefully about this offer of a post that few will be given a chance to take. Do you have any reason that you consider valid why you can't go to Germany to serve, not as a member of the armed forces, but in a civilian position?"

"What are the risks of going there as a civilian?"

"Obviously there are some Nazis that we haven't found yet, and perhaps some will never be found, but civilians are as protected as possible so the risks are small."

"In that case I'd be a fool if I didn't take the opportunity to use my linguistic skills for the nation. I'll get experience in using them that could be useful when I return to Britain."

"I'm glad to hear you say that. You are just the man we need, but there are others like you, of course. You'll have to go for training for a month. It will not be like the army, but there will be a basic course in self protection. Much of it will be preparation for going into a strange country and the rest will be learning about the work you'll be doing. You'll start at a low level, but with your qualifications you should soon rise to a higher one. How high I cannot say, but there are good opportunities there for someone, why not you? How good is your arithmetic?"

"Reasonable. I was never top of the class, but I always avoided being bottom."

"Then I'll recommend you for a position in the provision of food and other necessities for the civilian population. It may not be what you'll get, but there are good prospects in all fields for those who work hard. There is nothing better on offer in this country for you at this time. I said that you'll have to wait a while before you'll be allowed to marry. Is she British?"

"She's as English as I am."

"Good. You should be able to marry in about six months' time if your superiors think it wise at the time. You won't get army pay, nor will your marital status affect it in anyway. You'll start on a fairly low salary but after six months, if you are found to be satisfactory, you'll have sufficient pay to live comfortably with a wife and perhaps one child, but not yet enough to buy many luxuries.

"You'll serve a minimum of three years and there may be further opportunities after that time. It could be that if you climb high enough you may be offered a permanent position working for the Government, and believe me that's worth hoping for. Go home now, enjoy your lady's company, and we'll send details of where you must go for training."

George had been home five days when his new instructions arrived. He was given an address in the south of England where he would stay whilst receiving training for his work for the Government. As he was to remain a civilian he took some spare clothing to allow for laundry and changes in the weather.

A travel pass was provided, but this time it was only valid one way. Because he would be transferred to Germany immediately the course was completed he was allowed another week with his family before he had to present himself at the place of training.

During that week he and Alice spent as much time together as possible. Alec came home on leave for a few days during that week, and the two young men discussed the situation. Alec was very pleased that his brother wasn't to join the armed forces.

"I'm really glad that you won't be in the military. You're not the type of person who'd enjoy it. I'd never volunteer to be a soldier, but as it's peacetime I can manage to endure it. I'll be out in six months if they don't change their minds."

"Why do you think I wouldn't like it?"

"You're a more serious person who likes to do things properly. In the army you aren't a person, you're a piece of Government equipment to be used as the man above you dictates. He may be sensible, or he may be the biggest fool on the planet, it makes no difference. He represents the Government, and he uses you as he chooses, subject to the wishes of his superior."

"I'll have to obey orders in my position."

"Yes, but I think it'll be different. You'll be a civilian and military rules won't apply. Also you'll live better with more money in your pocket."

Alice wasn't happy when she learned that his freedom was coming to an end. "I'm going to miss you so very much. I agree with Alec that you're not cut out to be a soldier. You're too gentle for that. I only hope you'll not be in danger in Germany, they were our enemies quite recently."

"I don't have much fear of danger there. As I understand it the ordinary German looks on us as saviours. Really they were all slaves of the Nazis and never knew when a knock on the door in the middle of the night could come."

When the time came Alice took him to the station. He'd been learning how to drive her father's car, and had his last lesson with Alice before they parted.

"Oh, George," she said as they were about to part, "don't forget to write or telephone every week. I'll worry if I don't hear from you."

"I'll write as often as I can, and whilst I'm in Britain I'll telephone. I can't say about over there as I expect that the lines will be in a mess like everything else. I'm sad that I've to go so far from you and Mum and Dad, but I'm also excited because I'll get experience of working with my languages. From what Sir Alfred said it's a stepping stone to a good life afterwards. It'll be up to me to climb as high as I can in the next three years. The higher my position at the end and the better my chance of a good post either working for the Government or in private business."

The remainder of their time together was so private that we'll not report it. George boarded the train and prepared for a very long journey. When he arrived at the address he'd been given he found it was a large complex of Government buildings, including one for temporary accommodation for people like himself. He reported at Reception and was greeted courteously and asked to wait a few minutes after his details had been checked. Ten minutes later he was taken by a young girl to another building where a short gentleman with spectacles received him. He wore a blue suit and tie, and had a very precise manner of speech.

"Good afternoon, Mr. Briggs, and welcome to our establishment. Did you have a good journey?"

"Yes thank you, but it was a long one."

"In a few minutes I will send you to the accommodation allocated to you during your stay with us. Tomorrow you will begin a short course of training in self defence in the gymnasium in Block 2. It is not as severe as the police get, but it will be sufficient for most situations. You'll probably never need it, but they were the enemy and there could be some who still are. It's always best to be prepared. You'll be under the guidance of an ex-soldier, but you'll not be under army regulations. This training is solely for your own protection.

"After two weeks of this you'll have a couple of days learning about the life style you'll have over there, then we get down to your specific job. You'll be given a busy two weeks learning the basics of whatever job you are going to do. Then you'll be transferred to your working base in Germany where you'll be given extra details of your own job.

"It's up to you how well you learn and how efficient you become. Perhaps you'll feel disinclined to be an active member of the team, but that's not how to look at it. You are straight from college; there you'll learn how to be an employee. The same concepts apply both when working for the Government and in industry, or even as a teacher in a school. In the work you will be given you'll start at the bottom of the ladder. If you set your mind to climb it you'll be given every chance to use whatever talents you possess to build yourself a very lucrative career."

He spoke into a telephone and a young girl aged perhaps sixteen came into the room.

"Miss Smith, please take Mr. Briggs to Block 6 and help him to find out where he will sleep tonight."

"Yes sir," the girl replied, then she turned to George, "Please come with me, sir."

They left the building and walked about fifty yards to a huge brick building where the girl introduced her companion to a motherly looking woman with grey hair and a friendly smile.

"Welcome, Mr. Briggs. Your case has been taken to your room, now Miss Smith will guide you to it. Here is your key. When did you last eat?"

"On the train about noon."

"There's a restaurant in the next building, and it'll be open until seven o'clock. You also have facilities in your room for making tea or coffee."

"Thank you," George said as he left the room with the girl. He found that his room had a bed and a chair with basic furnishings for his clothes, and his case was by the bed.

After the girl had left he unpacked the case and put away his clothes and other items. He then locked his room and went to find the restaurant where he ate a good meal. Unlike the London canteen this food had to be paid for, but the prices were reasonable.

When his hunger had been satisfied he decided to get some fresh air after all those hours on the trains. He looked for the gymnasium he was to visit in the morning. The door was open when he found it, so he entered and found a young man working on some equipment. He stopped his exercises when he saw George.

"Hello, can I help you?" he asked.

"Hello. I've just arrived here and am trying to get a bit of fresh air on this beautiful day, and at the same time I want to find my way around. I've to come to this building tomorrow morning, so I decided to find it in advance. I'm supposed to have a short course in self defence."

"That means you'll be with Harry. This gym opens at 8.00am, so I suggest that you come then. He's a good fellow, and you should get on alright with him. Are you going abroad?"

"Yes, to Germany, I think."

"They give these lessons to all who go abroad unless they've been in the military or the police. It doesn't mean that you'll need it, but everyone gets it. Come in and ask for Harry in the morning."

"Thanks. I'll let you get on with your own thing now. Goodbye."

Next morning George went to the gymnasium early and soon found Harry. He was a well built fellow about thirty years old with short cropped hair and a ruddy complexion. He was an ex-army corporal.

"So you want the SD course? Right. Have you got shorts and vest?"

"Yes."

"I'll take your name and details before you change, and then we'll do some light exercises. Have you done much PT lately?"

"I haven't done any apart from walking."

"That's OK, we'll build it up gradually. This isn't the army so I'll not try to kill you on the first day."

"Thanks," George said with a grin.

During the next two weeks they loosened up George's muscles and the ex-soldier taught him how to deal with most of the ways that people are attacked.

"Now you should be able to look after yourself if you need it," Harry said on the last day.

George thanked him and returned to his room. There he found a sheet of paper had been delivered and it told him to attend a lecture in the morning of the next day and where it would be. It was given by an older man who seemed to be in his sixties or thereabout. He covered a lot of ground, speaking about Germany and the conditions there. He gave facts about the shops and the life of the population as well as the lack of amenities since the war ended. At the end he distributed a small handbook written to help workers to settle into their new environment.

"Study this and your notes of my talk, and be here at 10am tomorrow for a question and answer session. In the afternoon you'll have a period to write letters or do whatever you wish except leave and go home."

After the Q&A session that George thought very useful the short gentleman he had seen on the first day came into the room. He addressed the group of eight men and three women.

"Good morning. You have now ended the preliminary preparations. Tomorrow you will begin to individually train for the work you have been selected to do. Miss Baxter and Miss Wallace will be going to the same place and do similar work, so they can train together. Similarly Mr. Merritt and Mr. Johnson will stay together. The rest of you will each be treated separately. I suggest that everyone comes to this room at 9.00am when you will meet with your tutors and go with them to your lesson rooms."

George learned next day that his tutor was a smart, good looking young woman with naturally red hair, called Miss Walsh. She took him to a small room in which were four small tables with a chair by each.

"Please sit down, Mr. Briggs," she said as she moved a second chair to the table he had chosen. "We may as well sit facing each other for this first session. You may be surprised that I'm both young and a woman. Don't let it worry you. I've been doing the same work as you'll be doing in exactly the same district for two years. It's easy for an intelligent person, and there are good opportunities for promotion.

"I was offered this chance to come home for three weeks to train you and then have a week with my family. It also gives me a 20% rise in my salary. A week after you go to Germany I'll follow, but I don't yet know to which part. I'll have a higher rank than I left. Will promotion interest you when the time comes?"

"Very much so. Can you tell me where I'll be going, and what kind of work it will be?"

"Yes, your base will be Munich, but you'll have to move around all Bavaria to meet local officials and other people. You're considered an exceptional linguist so it won't be long before you get a chance to move to second grade with a rise in pay. Although you're sent by the Government you'll actually be working for a private company, doing Government work. You'll be working with the natives to try to get a smooth flow of food and other necessities to the German people.

"The first week you'll be in the area office in Munich studying the problems you'll have to solve. You'll have a month visiting towns with a more experienced person, probably a man, but not necessarily so. After that you'll be on your own. You're very lucky to be going there. South Bavaria is a beautiful country with many lakes, on which there is much wild life. I envy you in this one thing. I don't know where I'll be sent, but it isn't likely to be there. I hope that it's a similarly lovely place, as I love to watch wild life and enjoy the countryside. It's my favourite hobby."

"It's mine too, and that of my fiancé. What are the rules for sending letters and telephoning from there?"

"There are no restrictions on letters, but trying to find a telephone that works and get a line out of the country at the same time is difficult. Are you thinking of your fiancé?"

"Yes, and although my parents have no telephone they live close to her, and if it could be arranged they would go to her home to talk to me. I've used the box outside here."

"Is she pretty?"

"I think so, but of more importance she has similar interests to mine and a gentle personality."

"The rules are that you can marry after six months out there if your supervisor thinks that it's safe at the time. She can then come out to live with you there."

"That will be good."

During the time he was with her Miss Walsh gave him details of the type of problems he would have to deal with. Sometimes she'd act as the supplier, and he would have to chase up the goods that hadn't been delivered, though they'd been promised. On other days she would be a town official and he'd to help her to sort out local problems. All these sessions were carried out in German, but occasionally she'd pretend to be French and then his skill in that language would be used. No English was ever spoken during the lesson. Sometimes she set work for him to do in his room, making out reports of the progress or lack of it in the various situations he had to resolve.

He enjoyed the lessons and found his teacher a pleasant person to work with. By mutual consent they kept their conversation to the business of getting him ready to go to Germany. She was also engaged to be married, and they agreed that although it was good to be on a friendly footing it was sensible to limit their off duty association, though they did sometimes visit the restaurant together for lunch. The time passed very quickly, and George looked ahead with a hope of an interesting three years ahead.

CHAPTER 12

When George's last session with Miss Walsh was ending she informed him of his next move.

"On Monday you'll come here as usual and a car will take you to an R.A.F. airfield from where you'll fly to Munich, or Munchen as the Germans call it. Here is your travel pass that you'll have to show to various people. I wish you good luck and a happy time over there, and I hope that all goes well with your fiancé. I don't expect that we'll meet again, but who knows what those in command will decide? Goodbye."

She held out her hand and George took it in a farewell handshake. He later went to eat his evening meal. After that he telephoned Alice.

"This is it," he told her after they had greeted each other. "A car takes me to an airfield on Monday morning, from there I fly to Munich. The pilot will be taking some goods and papers and I get a free ride. I'm not too keen on going up in the air, but I suppose it'll be alright now."

"George, you must let me know when you've landed safely. Telephone if you can, but write quickly if that isn't possible. It's so awful that we'll be so far apart."

"I agree, but at least I'm a civilian, even though I'm tied for three years I'll be in a safe environment and getting more pay than a soldier. I'll get work experience with my German, and have a good chance of promotion."

On Monday morning he packed his belongings in his case and awaited the car. It arrived at 9.15 and after an hour the driver turned into an airfield. A sentry examined the passes of both George and the driver. He directed them to a nearby building where George left the car with his case. An officer scrutinised both the pass and his identity card.

"There is an aeroplane going to Munich at 11.30; it will take you. Have you ever flown before?"

"Never."

"Don't worry about it. They've stopped shooting at our stuff now, and the pilot has been flying a long time, at least six months. I suggest you might go to that building where the door is open and try to get a cup of tea."

"George did as the officer suggested and obtained a drink and a sandwich. As he ate the food he wondered what his life would be like in a foreign land that was enemy territory only a few years before.

"I wish I knew what lies ahead of me," he thought. "What will it be like over there? Will I get a good place to live? How will I get on with my colleagues and the Germans? I seemed to solve the problems Miss Walsh set me, but this will be the real thing."

At last a W.A.A.F. girl came and took him to where a small aeroplane was standing on the tarmac. A young man with a flying jacket was standing near it.

"You must be my passenger, Mr. Briggs."

"That's correct."

"I know half the population have looked at your pass and ID, but I've to see them as well," he said. George showed him the documents. "OK, put your case behind you and strap it in tight, then do the same thing for yourself. I've never lost a passenger yet and this crate has a lid on it, not like some I've flown. It can get bumpy, and I don't want to have to fill in a lot of forms because you get hurt."

The aeroplane took off and George was surprised how smoothly it left the ground. He was intrigued when it climbed the sky and he saw the panoramic views. It was a clear morning and the small amount of cloud was high and well broken. Soon he saw the sea below them.

"That land you see ahead is France," the pilot said into George's earphones. "We've a nice tail wind and are making good time." Later his voice came again, "How do you like flying?"

"It's nicer than I expected and the views are amazing."

"Those mountains you see in front of us are in Germany. We'll soon be there now."

The landing wasn't as smooth as the takeoff, and George was glad that he had the safety strap.

"Sorry about the bumps, but this strip hasn't been properly finished yet. There are so many things that need repairing or replacing after the bombing. All they could do is patch them up and go on to the next problem. We're on the ground now, so grab your case and come with me. I've to report to the airfield's commandant and you'll have to show your papers again, then we'll look for lunch. There's a good canteen here."

After they had eaten and George had thanked the airman a car took him into the city of Munich. It stopped before a building where he had to show his pass before entering its doors. A few minutes later he found himself seated in a small office facing a tall, distinguished gentleman with grey hair and wearing civilian clothes. He was about sixty years old and sitting behind a large desk.

"Mr. Briggs, welcome to our team. My name is Mr. Anderson. I understand you've met Miss Walsh whom you are replacing."

"Yes, she gave me some training for the work that I'm supposed to do here."

"Good. How do you feel about it?"

"If I've to be far from my family and friends it sounds as if it will be better than many alternatives. When do I start?"

"Tomorrow morning at 9.00, German time. Have you a watch?"

"Yes."

"Adjust it now. It's exactly 3.14 by our time here."

George made the alteration. "Have any arrangements been made for my lodgings tonight?"

"Yes, we've rented a room for you in a place owned by a widow called Frau Wirth. As you'll be working in this building for the first four weeks we've paid a month's rent. She'll provide bed and breakfast. If you wish her to see to your laundry you'll pay for it. Should you decide to keep the room after the four weeks you'll arrange it and pay the rent. A car will take you there after this interview is finished.

"Here are a local map and details of local public transport, but your lodgings are within walking distance of this building. Your salary will be paid monthly in arrears and in German money. Should you wish to send some home to your family or to take out a savings account we always recommend Deutsche Bundesbank. Remember that when it's changed into Sterling there'll be a fee, and the exchange rate can vary considerably."

He handed George a leaflet of bank literature and a form for opening an account. An assistant came into the room and told them the car was waiting, and Mr. Anderson asked her to take George to it.

"Come to this office tomorrow, and don't forget to bring your pass or you'll not get into the building," he reminded George before he left.

Very soon after leaving its underground parking place the car pulled up outside a row of houses with small gardens in front of them.

"Here you are, sir," the driver said. "I'll just wait to make sure that you get in."

"Thank you."

The driver grabbed the case and walked to the door. He rang the bell and a fair haired woman who looked to be about forty opened the door.

"Good afternoon, Frau Wirth," the driver greeted her in German. "This is Herr Briggs for whom you have a room reserved."

"Come in, Herr Briggs, and welcome to Munchen."

George relieved the driver of the case and thanked him before following the woman into the house.

"Would you like a cup of coffee or tea whilst we have a little talk?"

"Yes, please." He was glad that he was now using his education in a real life situation instead of the various tests he'd experienced. A few minutes later he was facing the widow and sitting in a comfortable chair. They both had cups of coffee and he had two plain biscuits.

"This is the lounge used by the residents," she told him. "Your people have paid rent for four weeks for you to have the room I will show you shortly, and for breakfast every morning. That is all they will pay for. If you wish me to do your laundry, or you want to stay longer, you will pay for that. Have you been to Germany before?"

"No, I just arrived today. Until now I've never been out of England."

"At the moment I have six of your people here, so you'll make it seven. You'll meet them at breakfast, unless you see them in this room tonight. Now I'll show you your room."

She led him up a flight of stairs to a small room with a single bed and the usual basic furniture. A well worn carpet covered the floor and in the corner were a toilet and a wash bowl. Tea making equipment was near a window that looked out on the street. There was also a small wireless set.

"There's a bathroom on the landing between this floor and the one above. I know some things need changing, but it's impossible to buy carpets and things like that."

"I'm sure I'll manage," George told her as he thought of all the privations they had experienced when his father was unemployed.

After Frau Wirth went downstairs George unpacked his case and put away his clothes. He then got out the map and studied it for a while. Frau Wirth only provided breakfasts so he decided to explore the area and find something to eat. He locked his room and put the keys that his landlady had given him into his pocket before leaving the building. He'd changed some money into marks in England, so he looked for a café that was open and reasonably priced.

There seemed to be plenty of places to eat so he chose one that had a menu he thought would satisfy him without costing too much. The food was plain but well cooked; it was the kind that he preferred. He made a note of the street and the name of the café for future reference and then strolled through the district before returning to his lodgings. As he walked he noticed several churches, some of them looked very old and had interesting architecture and ornamentation on them.

When he arrived at his new home he felt rather weary, so he wrote a short note for Alice and one for his parents to travel in the same envelope, then he retired to bed. After a good sleep in a comfortable bed he arose and soon went downstairs to the breakfast room where he found four young men and two young ladies already seated at a long table.

"Ah, here he is," one of the men declared. "I presume you're the man from England."

"Yes, my name is George Briggs, and I flew in yesterday."

"Welcome, George, I'm Robert Harrison, better known as Bob. Going around the table from me are Tom Bell, Peter Fanshaw, Eric Cooper, Eileen Meakin and Pauline Rhodes."

"Yes, welcome from all of us," Tom Bell said. "We always speak English amongst ourselves. Frau Wirth is very good to us, so when she's around we make it easier for her and use German."

"Are you going in to work this morning?" Eric asked. "If you are it would be best to go with us, then we can show you the shortest way and point out some useful shops and the pub we use."

"Thank you. I've to be there for nine o'clock."

"We all have," Eileen said, "and they don't like lateness."

"Which department are you in?" Pauline asked.

"Something to do with supplies for the natives."

"Then you are replacing Nancy Walsh," Peter said.

"Yes, we met in England and she said that I was to take over her area."

"So long as you don't try to take her over," Eileen said. "She's engaged to Bob, and he's unhappy because she's going to pastures new."

"He can have Miss Walsh with my good wishes. I've my own girl, and she's also unhappy because I'm here."

When they had all eaten a hearty breakfast they returned to their rooms for various items before meeting in the lounge to walk to work together. As Eric had proposed they pointed out useful shops, cafes and the pub. At ten minutes to nine George entered the building, and his presence was recorded. Shortly after he'd returned to the room where he'd met Mr. Anderson the man walked in.

"Good morning, Mr. Briggs. Was your accommodation satisfactory? By the way, I'm head of all parts of this branch of the rehabilitation of Germany. You're scheduled to be in this building for a week. You'll work in a small room, most of the time alone. I'll give you a folder of reports of problems solved by your predecessor, Miss Walsh. Study them, see how she handled them and also the companies and authorities she dealt with. That will give you some idea of your own duties. On Saturday morning I'll check your understanding of the job, and if I think you're ready you'll go out into the wide world next week.

"Of course you'll have another person with you for a while to make sure that you don't get lost or bewildered by what you have to deal with. We often understand something until we have to start to do it, then it becomes harder. Of one thing I can assure you, you'll have it easier than Miss Walsh had at first, and the person before her had only half of the territory that she had. Things were very difficult then, but we're getting on top of it now. Soon the Germans will take this work off our hands when they get their own Government.

"I don't yet know who'll accompany you in those first weeks. Miss Walsh is still in England, and it's expected that she'll be moved elsewhere. We did request that she be allowed to stay here near her fiancé, but I'll be very surprised if we get her back."

He took George to the room where he would work and gave him a note pad, a fountain pen and the folder of past cases.

"Here you are. Try to get the feel of the problem. It'll be worth your while. Apart from your £30 per month we've a bonus scheme that depends on your ability to keep things running smoothly. There are also opportunities for promotion from time to time, and I try to see to it that the conscientious worker is the one who moves up the ladder. Remember this is a civilian company working for the Allies; after the three years you have to do it may be profitable to stay with us.

"I'm of the Company, but I'm in charge of other things done from this office. Of course once the Germans take over there'll be nothing for any of us here, but both the British Government and the Company have other concerns beside this one. When you move into the field you'll need a car. Do you drive?"

"I've a provisional licence, the only one available in Britain at present. My fiance's father took me out in his car a few times, and later I drove when I was out with her, but I haven't been to cities much. If it's possible I think it would be best if I could go out with an experienced German and get tuition on German roads. Here they drive on the right and all the signs are different."

"Yes, you're very wise to want to do this. I'll set up something for you and let you know what I arrange. As you're not part of a team as some here are I suggest that you take a lunch hour from noon to one o'clock this week. When you're on the road you'll find you've to adapt to whatever circumstances are there at the time. Sometimes you've to fit in with the needs of others. For today there's a very good café just across the street, and it has reasonable prices. Now I'll leave you to your studies."

George opened the folder and began looking through its contents. As he did so he realised what a good teacher Miss Walsh had been. Many of the cases were similar to the problems she'd given him to solve. He soon devised a system for filing the names of town officials, suppliers and those supplied. He used several pages of his pad for this in the hope that it would simplify his work in a new job in a new country.

All week he worked diligently and by Friday afternoon he felt that he had a working knowledge of how to go about solving people's problems. The next morning he was waiting when Mr. Anderson entered the room. For two hours he tested George with hypothetical difficulties in various parts of Bavaria. He was impressed when George referred to his notes on people in different areas and positions.

"Now you're ready for the road. I've arranged for you to go with one of our most experienced drivers this afternoon. Go out now and have an early lunch, then come back to meet Johann at the front desk at 1.00pm. He's a German who works for us from time to time, and he's willing to help you. He'll show you your car and take you out. We'll pay for his time so you've no worries there. If he wants to take you out tomorrow it's alright with us, if you don't object to Sunday work."

"Thank you. When will I meet my colleague for next week?"

"Monday morning, I hope. You know as much as I do at the moment."

After lunch George met Johann who was a broad shouldered man of medium height with fair hair and a scar down the left side of his face that spoiled what would have been a handsome one. He took George to the garage under the building and led him to a black saloon car.

"This is your car," he said in his own language. "We'll go out for a ride and see how you adjust to driving on the right. Once you get used to all the instruments being the other way around and sitting on the other side of the car it will be simple. How long have you been driving?"

"Not very long. It wasn't my car, and the owner could only spare a certain amount of petrol. I've driven in a city, but only three times."

"I will teach you."

Johann took the car out of the city, then he stopped and George took over the wheel. They spent about three hours driving around country lanes and rather busier roads, and at the end Johann was willing to let George drive into the city and back to the garage.

"You are doing very well, but I want to take you out tomorrow morning for a while. The autobahn will be quiet early on a Sunday and I want to take you there. For ordinary roads you are safer than many, but the autobahn is different. I suggest that you don't use it unless there is no alternative for a while. If you do have to use it try not to do so in the rush hour. Meet me at 9.00 in the morning at the office."

George thanked him and walked home for a well earned rest. Sunday morning was fine and sunny as they left the car park. George was at the wheel and he drove out of the city without any criticism from his companion. They came to the entrance to one of the busiest roads in Bavaria. Johann took over the wheel.

"I'll drive for a while and show you the things you'll need to know. Later, when we come to a service station we'll change seats and you'll drive in the slow lane for a while."

They did as he had said and had no difficulty. There was some traffic, but not as much as there would be during the week. Later at the garage George thanked him.

"I'm glad that I was able to help you," Johann said in reply. "You are doing alright, but take it carefully. Keep off the autobahn unless it is absolutely necessary. There is usually a quieter road."

Monday morning found George in the main office wondering what kind of a person his new instructor would be. They would be together for a month and sometimes it would be impossible to return to Munich the same day. He was sitting with his brief case and file of information when he heard a woman's footsteps in the corridor. To his amazement Nancy Walsh walked through the door.

"Hello. What a surprise, you said that you expected to have to go somewhere else."

"I did, but I'm lucky. Mr. Anderson requested that I remain in this section as I'm engaged to Bob, and he's pulled it off. I only got to know yesterday, so it has been a rush to get here for today."

"What will you do now I have your old job?"

"First of all I've a month with you, then I'll be your supervisor and that of others. I'm lucky, not just because I'll be with Bob. This is a lovely time of year for bird life. Bob and I'll be out most weekends, and he's agreed to take you with us a few times to show you the best places to go.

"We'll only go to one problem today, and that's here in Munich, then we'll spend the rest of the day looking at maps of the districts you'll have to cover and get you familiar with this city. I hear you have been out with Johann a couple of times."

"Yes, I hadn't driven much, and never in a left hand drive or on one of these roads. He's been very helpful, and I think that you'll be fairly safe with me now."

"Good, it was a wise move. Tom has been holding the fort whilst I was with you in England. Now he'll have more time for his own job and you'll do this one, with me there watching and ready to help if you need it. I suppose that you've heard that my first name is Nancy, and I know that yours is George. I know you a little better now and we'll be together a lot, especially this first month, both at work and at the lodgings. I suggest that we reduce the formality and use first names, unless our bosses are around. Do you agree?"

"Certainly, I think we can each trust the other. You have Bob and I have Alice, though she's too far away. I see no need for a lot of formality, and it'll be nicer working together as friends. It'll be easier when the others are there as well."

"Good, now we'll prepare for your first real problem as opposed to the ones you've been working on up to now."

CHAPTER 13

Nancy passed to George a document like those he had seen during his training. It told the name of the organisation where difficulties were being experienced. In this case it was a hospital in Munich. Their stock of anaesthetics was very low. An order had been sent to the supplier and reminders had followed but the goods hadn't arrived. Unless a delivery came quickly operations would have to be suspended. The supplier was a French firm with a depot in Stuttgart.

"First of all you need to know where the hospital is," Nancy told George. "It'll be a wise move to go there as this is your first contact with them. Knowing your contacts personally is useful whenever possible, and as this one is here in this city it should be easy."

George got out his map of Munich and soon found the hospital. He then planned his route through the streets. When he thought he had a good one Nancy looked at it and made one alteration.

"I always try to avoid that area if I can. There are more traffic problems there than in any other part of the city."

She adjusted the route to avoid the possible congestion and they went out to George's car. They arrived at the hospital without any difficulty. George had telephoned for an appointment, so they had only a short time to wait before the person in charge of supplies came to them. Nancy knew him and introduced George as her replacement and the two men shook hands.

"We've a crisis looming up unless we get our supplies," George was told. "We ordered at the right time and have both written and telephoned, but still we haven't got our goods. Unless the anaesthetics arrive by the weekend there will be no surgical work done next week."

"Are you sure there's no problem about finance? Did you pay for the last lot and get confirmation that they'd got the money? Sometimes things can go wrong in the post."

"Yes, I've a receipt for it in my office."

"It seems you've had difficulties with this French firm before."

"Unfortunately that is true."

"I think the best thing is for me to contact them and try to find out why there is a problem. If they can't supply immediately I'll try to get you temporary relief from the Americans. You should have some sort of a supply by Thursday. If you haven't please telephone our office, and if I'm not there leave a message for me or Miss Walsh."

"You handled that very well," Nancy said when they returned to the car. "Now what will you do?"

"I checked my file before we came out. This company are rather lax with their promises so I'll contact M. Oudinot, the manager, to see what can be done. If he can't supply immediately I'll try the American depot. It may mean that we have to find another supplier if the French cannot improve their performance. The first priority is to keep those surgeons working."

"Your filing system seems to be working very well. If you've to get another source I've more information than you have yet. All you have are the firms you gleaned from what we gave you in the lessons. Always come to me if you're in need of more information. I'm very impressed by the knowledge you have already. Now I think that we've earned our lunch, and there is a little place where I always go if I'm on this side of the city. It's close by and I hope that you'll like it. That's another subject for your file, how to avoid starvation on the job."

During the afternoon George telephoned the supplier and Nancy was surprised by his fluency in French as it was almost equal to his German. She listened on an extension and liked his manner of dealing with M. Oudinot. His excuse was late delivery from their factory near Paris. He said they had received a delivery that morning and George obtained a promise that the Munich order would be despatched that day by urgent express delivery.

"That was very well dealt with," Nancy commented after George had informed the hospital of the promise he'd obtained. He also told them to let him know if the goods didn't arrive next day.

The remainder of the afternoon was spent by George and Nancy studying maps of Bavaria, charts showing the location of suppliers of goods and other information. The afternoon passed pleasantly, and at the end of it they walked to their lodgings with Bob. Nancy was returning to the accommodation she'd used before she went to England. During the next four weeks George and Nancy went out together to different parts of the state every Monday to Friday. Saturday mornings were normally kept for making out reports and George used them to update his files as he obtained more information.

The first Sunday was stormy and none of the nature lovers went abroad. George wrote to his family, and a long letter to Alice. The following week the weather was much better. George was told to be ready to leave at 6.30 to set off to a valley some distance away. He had a wonderful day out and saw several birds and other creatures new to him. He made notes so that he could describe the day to Alice in his next letter. On three other occasions he was taken to different places of beauty and interest and Bob told him of several more.

"I don't think I need to intrude on your time together any more," he told his friends after the fourth outing. "With the information you've given me, Bob, and various leaflets, I've quite a variety of places to visit. Thank you both for your help. Both Alice and I will enjoy finding out about these new creatures."

At the end of their four weeks of travelling together on the problem solving journeys Nancy came to George on the Saturday morning.

"You'll be going out alone from now on as you are aware. Don't hesitate to come to me if you find a situation that's too difficult for you to solve. I've made my first report on your progress for Mr. Anderson and those above him, and I'm glad to say that it's a positive one. Things are slowly changing here in Germany as you're aware. The Allies are still in power, but gradually more responsibility is being given to the German leaders. Different responsibilities will be passed to them, and some of us will go home.

"Already we've Germans doing work like yours in different parts of the country. Eventually they'll take over all the front line work of keeping things flowing, but the people in Bonn have said that for some time after they take over control of Government they would like a few to stay to help during the early period."

"Will you be one of them?"

"Definitely not. Unlike you Bob and I aren't conscripts. We both worked for the Company before the British Government ask for its help. I can resign at any time and return to England. You've a fairly long time to serve, I see good opportunities for you if you want them. Both Bob and I have contracts that terminate in December, and we plan to go home and marry. Bob will take a new post with the Company in Britain, and by spring we should be settled in our own home. You're very good at your work, and your linguistic abilities are rare. If you continue to be as successful as I think you will I'll try to get you my job when I leave.

"I now control our people doing your job over a quarter of the country. British, American and German men and women work under my supervision. I am based in this building, but will sometimes have to travel. I'll let you know how to contact me when I go in case you need help, but try to manage as much as you can for the sake of the future.

"If I can show that you can work with the minimum supervision it'll help me to speak for you to Mr. Anderson later. I want you to get this job, you're already better organised than most of the others, and you're just starting. Your ability to speak with Germans and French will be a strong point in your favour. You've time to prove yourself to Mr. Anderson before December, so stick at it and I'll do my best for you. If you get my job you are half way to getting the job with the German Government when it takes over."

"Will I be allowed to transfer to them as I'm under our Government's control?"

"Yes, if you go to the Germans you'll be officially on loan from the Company, even when you're still under British Government control. You'll be able, when both Governments have finished with you, to return to the Company either here or in Britain or somewhere else, and get another position with it at the most recent level. All this is ahead of you if you try hard enough. There's no limit to the potential; it will be up to you once you convince Mr. Anderson that you're worth it."

"Thank you, Nancy. You've only known me for a little over two months, so this is unexpected. I'll do this job to the best of my ability, and try not to build up to much hope. Whatever happens I appreciate your help and wish you and Bob great happiness in England."

George had very little difficulty in keeping the wheels turning in the hospitals and other users of his services through out Bavaria. Only twice did he have to get help from Nancy, and for one of them she had to turn to Mr. Anderson.

Meanwhile he enjoyed visiting the wild life places they'd shown him, as well as others he had found. He saw many creatures new to him and they filled a large part of his letters. When he was at Cambridge he'd reported to Alice about the bird life of the Fens, so he was able to send long and interesting letters every week about what he saw in this foreign land.

Every now and again he got a few free days, so on those occasions he left Bavaria to explore other parts of the country. His only regret was that Alice couldn't be there with him. When he could he arranged a time for a telephone call. Some member of his family would be with Alice to hear his voice and speak to him.

As Christmas drew near and Nancy was getting ready to leave he wondered if she'd been able to get her job for him. He'd seen a German in the building and feared that he might be taking over, but on the Saturday before the first week in December Nancy came to him.

"On Monday you'll not go out. Franz will be taking over your area. You'll be taking over my job running one quarter of the country with seven agents under you. You'll receive another pay rise, 50% more than you're getting now. You're doing well, because you work hard and can speak both German and French so well it's been easy for me to get you on the ladder of success. Next week you'll familiarise yourself with my documents and I'll take Franz out to show him your section. He should only need a week as he's from Nurenburg and knows all the state very well."

"You did it! You got your job for me! Thank you very much."

"It wasn't difficult. Very few British can speak the language really well. You were taught by a German, and it shows. I'm very pleased for you, and so are Bob and Mr. Anderson. Now have you any plans for Christmas?"

"How can I have when I'm here?"

"How about a trip to see Alice?"

"That's too nice to think about."

"Right, I'll arrange it. There'll be very little activity here during that week. Telephone her and tell her to expect you on the 23rd."

George couldn't get to a telephone quickly enough when his work was finished. By now there wasn't as much pressure on the system, so he got through fairly quickly, only to learn that Alice was visiting a friend who'd broken her leg.

"I'm sorry, George, can I give her a message?" Mrs. Shepherd asked.

"Yes please, get her and my mother to the telephone tomorrow at eleven o'clock, your time. I've very important special news."

"I'll arrange it, George. Is it good or bad news? Are you alright?"

"I was alright at breakfast, now I'm wonderful, and Alice will be tomorrow, I promise you."

+ + +

"Hello, is that you, George?"

"It certainly is, darling."

"Mum says that you have good news. Are you returning to England?"

"I'll be home on the 23rd and will stay until New Year's Day."

"It's not for keeps then?"

"No, but I'll definitely get Christmas at home. Is Mother there?"

"Yes, here she is."

"Hello, George. Are you alright?"

"Very much so at present, but unless you feed me at Christmas I may not be."

"Are you coming home?"

"I've a week with you, thanks to Nancy. She and Bob are coming home to stay and marry, and I get her job in the New Year with a 50% pay rise."

"That's wonderful. Now I'll give you back to Alice."

"I'm back again, love. How did you get the time off?"

"Nancy did it. She's coming home with Bob to stay. She got her job for me and arranged this leave. She's a real pal. They're free members of the Company's staff, not like me. I'm employed by the Company, but put there by the British Government. We'll all fly together. Bob lives in Manchester when he's in Britain, so we'll fly there together."

"Let me know when you expect to land and I'll borrow Dad's car and fetch you."

CHAPTER 14

As Christmas approached George and the others who lived at Frau Wirth's lodgings began to make plans. A few would stay on duty to cover any emergencies, not just in the logistics department but in all matters dealt with in the building. George was to fly with Robert Harrison and Nancy Walsh to Manchester. Tom Spencer and Pauline Rhodes had arranged to fly together to London where they both had families. On the morning of the 21st Frau Wirth came into the breakfast room.

"My friends, I am speaking mainly to the group from the English office, but all are included. There are only two of you, but you are my lodgers just as the English are. I find that five of you will not be here over Christmas and two are not coming back. I have made plans for us to have a meal together. Will you all be able to dine here tomorrow evening?"

After some discussion Eric said, "This is very kind of you, Frau Wirth. All our people can be here any time after seven o'clock. Herr Strauss says that he'll be with friends tomorrow night, but he thanks you for the invitation. Herr Schmidt will join us. We don't know him, but we hope to after tomorrow. That means there'll be nine of us beside yourself. Is there anything that you wish us to bring?"

"No, all is taken care of. I have no family in Bavaria, you are all that I have here, and I want to enjoy a meal with you. The food will be ready at 7.30. As most of you are British I will try to cook a British meal with a turkey and Christmas pudding. I have wine, both red and white, not enough to get you drunk but enough to enjoy together."

"I also wish to thank you for your kind offer, Frau Wirth," Herr Schmidt said. "Like the other man said we can all get to know each other over good food and wine."

After all had eaten the eight companions met in Bob's room and Herr Schmidt was invited to join them for a few minutes.

"We have asked you to join us so that you can hear what we discuss, Herr Schmidt," Bob said, " The Frau has treated all our people well, and now she's putting on this meal for us. Some of us feel that we would like to give her a present from the group. You may not feel this concerns you, but as you will be there when the present is given we invite you to be included if you wish."

"Certainly I will join. I think it is most kind of the lady. I see it is intended mainly for your group, but she has invited me. I will be pleased to be part of this giving of a present. Whatever you agree amongst yourselves I will equally contribute."

Tom spoke first. "As they are leaving early on the morning after the meal Bob, Nancy and George will have spare time tomorrow, so I suggest that they decide what the gift should be, and purchase it. If we all put in an agreed sum they can work to that. If it costs more we'll cover it later, if there's some left we'll give the spare to a charity. Do you all agree to that idea? If you do what figure should we work with?"

All agreed and a sum was decided. Each gave a share including Herr Schmidt, whose first name was Theo.

The evening was a wonderful success. The meal was excellent, and Frau Wirth had cooked it well. Bob and Nancy had selected a beautiful clock for her.

"Thank you for that delicious food, Frau Wirth," Eric said. "All here have asked me to express our gratitude for the kind thought behind it. Now we have a little gift for you from all of us here including Theo. Eileen, will you give it to her please?"

When she had opened the parcel their hostess was ecstatic. "Thank you all very much. What a beautiful clock! I will always treasure it. I have never received a present since my husband was killed until now."

Next morning Frau Wirth had an early breakfast for the travellers and when it was eaten Eileen Meakin took the Manchester group to the airport in George's car for a 9.20 flight. It was considered safer for her to take them and park the car in the garage rather than leave it at the airport over the holiday. Bob and Nancy gave their addresses to George, and he gave them his as well as the telephone number of the mill house. They all agreed that they wanted to stay in touch with each other.

After a smooth flight over a countryside covered by snow they crossed the Channel and landed safely at Manchester Airport. When all formalities had been dealt with the trio came through to the public area. Alice was waiting and she threw her arms around George. Bob's sister was less demonstrative as she greeted her brother and his fiancé.

"Thank God you got here safely," Alice said. "You're looking well; that Frau Wirth must be looking after you properly."

"She looks after us all well. She put on a wonderful meal for us last night because five of us won't be there over the holiday and Bob and Nancy will stay in England now."

"I wish that you had come home to stay."

"Yes, and so do I, but as I can't we must look on the bright side. Whilst I'm there I can climb higher up the ladder. When I come home I'll have proved that I can carry the responsibility and will have a better chance of a good job here. Here come Bob and Nancy to meet you and see that you really are the nice person they have heard about."

George introduced his friends to Alice, and Bob did the same for his sister Joyce.

"I think that you're the lady George has been working with," Alice said."

"I was his superior, now he'll be doing my job. I feel sure that he'll be a success in it, and we hope that he'll go even higher before long. We didn't really expect him to get the job, because he hasn't been over there long, but he has better German than any of us, and he's a good man at the work."

"He's wonderful in every way."

"That's what he says about you. Bob and I have been eager to meet such a marvellous person."

"Yes," Bob added, "there's a girl there called Pauline who is very nice, but lonely. When he first joined us she offered him friendship in a proper way to help him settle and give her a friend. He gently told her about you, and she thanked him for the kind way he declined her offer."

When they were crossing the Pennines in the car Alice asked George about the women in the office.

"How many women work at your office?" she asked.

"I'm not sure. We've Pauline and Eileen in our office, and I know we've a few Germans in the typing pool. I've not spent a lot of time in the building as yet because most of my work was out in the field travelling all over Bavaria. Now that I have Nancy's job I'll be at base much more, but when I do go out it'll be over a much wider territory. I may need to use one of the typists sometimes now; I'm not sure how busy I'll be. It's a great opportunity, and I only got it through the help of Nancy. She worked on Mr. Anderson and now he's keen for me to get the next step that'll come soon.

"The Germans will take over our work before long, and he'll come home with most of the people, but they want about three of us over the whole country to stay and help them to take over smoothly. Mr. Anderson wants me to get one of those positions."

"Do you mean that you'll have to stay to work for the Germans?"

"Yes, if I'm lucky enough to get it. My three years will still not be up when it starts, so I may as well be doing what I know for them rather than something I know nothing about. The money will increase again, and that's good. Sir Alfred said the sky was the limit to my opportunities, and so far it seems that I'm climbing like a rocket. When I do come home I can return to the company and land another job on a par with what I'm earning when I leave the Germans. But I've still to get it. Mr. Anderson will do his best, but the final choice will be made by the new employers, the Germans."

When Alice stopped the car outside the Briggs home Gwen came out followed by Alec, who was now a civilian and taking a break for Christmas. William was on duty at the hotel. Gwen was pleased to see that her son was both healthy and happy. It was the first time that she had seen him since he went to

Germany. Some of the neighbours noticed him and came out to welcome him home, but Richard and Helen were at their office.

They went into the cottage and Alice looked around with interest. She had never been in any of the poor people's homes, and she wondered how four adults could be happy in such a small dwelling. Gwen made some tea and all enjoyed that with her baked luxuries, as well as the return of her elder son. After a short while Alice said that she must return her father's car as he might need it. George went outside with her.

"I'm so happy to see you looking so well. When you have satisfied your family's immediate needs I hope that you'll come to our house for the evening."

"I'll come after tea. Mum won't be satisfied until she has seen me eat a meal."

+ + +

When he arrived at the mill house Walter was there. After he and his wife had greeted George Alice claimed him and took him into the lounge.

"He'll only be here just over a week, so I want him as much as possible, and now's the best time to start," she told her parents.

Once they were alone she asked him about his work and the new job he would have on his return. "Will this new job cause you to have to travel more?"

"Not much more once I know my people, but as a bit of a boss I should try to get to know them and give them a chance to know me. There's a bonus in the travel as I'll be able to see new parts of the country. Germany has many beautiful areas with a lot of wild life we don't see here. There are bears, deer, chamois, wildcat and many other mammals, but I don't know which I'll have in my new area. It'll be interesting as I find out. I wish you could see them with me."

"So do I. Could I come for a visit?"

"I don't see any reason why you can't. I was going to suggest it. If I have to stay over there a long time I wondered about us marrying whilst I'm working there. It's as safe there as here now."

"That would be wonderful, we must discuss it more fully before you go back."

Before he went home Walter and Edith spoke to him. "George, do you think that we could get your family here for dinner on Boxing Day? Ernest is coming with Dorothy tomorrow, so if we can arrange it we would like all of you the day after."

"I'll see what I can do, but Dad may not be able to get time off. This is a busy period for the hotel trade. As I've only just got here I don't know what Alec's plans are."

"Do the best you can, and be here yourself whatever other people do."

"Thank you. Now I must go and get some sleep. We were up early this morning to catch the plane. Goodnight all."

Alice saw him off the premises with some private words of her own. Next morning George and Alice went to the hide and spent a short while there. It was a very cold morning with a keen frost and some snow on the ground. Part of the dam was frozen and they watched the mallards and other birds around the open water.

When they had seen the few creatures that were there they decided to walk into Cullerton as they had done so many times to catch the train. Walking soon warmed them, and they had a chance to be together with no interruptions from other people. It brought many memories for George of his school days when they passed the first school he attended.

"Shall we call on Mr. and Mrs. Pighills?" George asked. "I would like to see him again. He was always a good friend as well as a teacher."

Alice agreed and they went to the retired teacher's home.

"Well, what a surprise," Mrs. Pighills exclaimed when she opened the door. "Come in. Charles, look who's here."

"So you survived in the land of the enemy," Mr. Pighills greeted George. "And you, Alice, are you happy now he's returned?"

"Only to a degree, as he's to go back next week. I'm going to keep him by me as much as possible whilst he's here."

"I don't blame you," Mrs. Pighills said, "but remember that his family will want to see a lot of him too."

"Could you visit him in Germany?" her husband asked.

"We have been discussing that," George told him. "I think that Frau Wirth would be happy to have her for as long as she wants to stay, and Bavaria is a lovely state for her to visit. You called them the enemy, but that is over. Most Germans were glad to see the end of the Nazis."

Nellie made some tea and they ate mince pies with it. When it was time to set off home for lunch George asked Mr. Pighills, "Before I return to Germany can you find time for a talk with me about my future? I'll be over there for at least two years, it may be more. Sooner or later I'll come home, and I need to plan ahead."

"Of course I can find time; sometimes there's too much of it. What about the day after Boxing Day? Bring Alice with you and have lunch with us. We don't get as much young company as we'd like. We'll end up old before our time if we aren't careful."

"Yes, that sounds a good idea," his wife said. "Whilst you men discuss the important things of the future Alice can tell me how she manages to spend her days without you."

On the way home Alice asked, "Why do you want Mr. Pighills' advice? I thought that you were going to stay with the Company."

"At present it looks to me to be a good way to go, but your father and Mr. Pighills are older and more experienced. I would like to hear their views. It's a long way ahead but we need to be thinking now."

The whole week was a pleasure for the lovers. There was a dance at the hotel on Christmas Eve. They went to it and enjoyed the company of Helen and

Richard. Constance was there, and she was glad to have been allowed back. William was on duty with Elsie, and everybody was happy and in a party mood.

Alec had already arranged to go with other young people on Boxing Day, so he asked his father to apologise to the Shepherds. William was free until evening when there was another activity in the hall, but George and his parents enjoyed a good lunchtime meal and conversation with Alice's parents.

George discussed his future with both his old teacher and the mill owner before he returned to Germany. Both thought that it would be wisest to come back to England as an employee of the Company. If he got the position with the new German Government he would still be counted as one of theirs, and a job would be found for him when it was needed. With Bob and Nancy pushing for him he could land a very good position without any difficulty. If what was offered wasn't satisfactory he could look around after he got home for something else, but he wouldn't be unemployed like his father had been.

When he returned to Munich he soon settled into his new job without any difficulty. It was really the same as he had before, but now others ran around and he spent more time in the office and supervised. He showed each of his team the filing system he'd devised and most of them decided to use it. Nancy had left him plenty of new information, and he felt comfortable with his responsibility.

He tried to meet one or more of his team each week, which meant that he was away from Munich at least one day every week. He now had all the south of the land right across to the French border. When he found that he had the Black Forest region he was delighted as it gave him a much more varied territory. As he moved around he saw different kinds of scenery, and was able to combine it with the visits to his team members.

He arranged with Mr. Anderson that when he knew in advance that he would have to go somewhere special he would go on the Saturday afternoon and have Sunday to see the wild life. Any cover for his absence would be on the Monday. It didn't often happen that such cover would be needed, but it gave George a freedom he much enjoyed.

It was decided that Alice would come to Munich for a holiday at Easter. George would have an extra day of free time, and be able to show her enough of the city for her to be able to amuse herself when he was at work. Frau Wirth was pleased to let her have a room for her stay, and when she came she soon settled down in the small group of George's friends. Whilst he was at the office she explored the city and found much to interest her. If he went to meet an agent she went with him to see more of the country.

Frau Wirth was thrilled because she was there and able to talk with her in German, though she wasn't as fluent as George. As the landlady said, the more she used her German and the better she would speak it. When the time came for her to leave Frau Wirth was nearly as sad as George; she didn't have many friends, and had enjoyed Alice's company. She gave her some good advice.

"You must get married. Don't wait until he can live in England. You need to be together whilst you are still young. You don't know what fate has for you ahead. My husband and I thought we would have many years of happiness and we only got two before they made him go on the Russian Front and he was killed. Grab what you have while you still have it. Marry him and live here. He has a long time to stay yet. Do not waste it."

"I fully agree," George said. "We need to be together. This short holiday has shown that it can be done."

"It's alright for a week or two wandering around Munich when you are at the office, George, but what would I do every day of every week? Where would we live; these are all single rooms?"

"I can answer that last part for you," Frau Wirth told her. "I have a friend who has a lot of furnished apartments or flats as you English call them. They are good, and not too expensive. If you want me to I'll enquire if she has one coming vacant in the near future. Even if she hasn't she'll know other owners. You would then have the flat to care for, shopping to do, and you have enough German to take on a part-time job, either for a wage or to help a charity."

"That makes it sound a lot better," Alice said. "We'll have to think about it; we do want to be together if it's at all possible."

The evening before she was to return home George took her for a short walk beside the River Isar. They sat on a seat and watched several boats sailing by.

"I wish that I didn't have to leave you tomorrow," Alice said.

"I know; I wish it too. As I'll be here for at least twenty more months perhaps we should do as the frau says. If she can get us a decent flat we'll be at least half way to happiness."

"We need to think about it and decide as soon as we can."

"The best thing I can think of at present is for me to have a talk with Mr. Anderson and see what he thinks. I have to get his sanction in any case as I'm government property and he's responsible to them for me. If he thinks it's wise, and he's been here a long time, I'll go to see Frau Wirth's friend and look at her flats, and others if I need to. I'll put it all in a letter and then we can talk on the telephone. If I send the letter first we'll not forget to mention anything as we talk. Also if it's in a letter you can show it to your parents and discuss it with them if you wish.

"You'd be safe here; most of these people see us as their rescuers. I haven't heard of one of our people being assaulted. As we'll be living in Munich, at least until the Germans take over the work, you'll have Frau Wirth to give you advice about the best shops and other things. She's a very nice person."

"Yes love, make those enquiries; I like what I've seen of the country and its wild life. That family of wild pigs we saw was lovely, but I wouldn't like the boar to be angry with me. See what we can do; I so much want to be with you."

George sought an interview with Mr. Anderson the day after Alice left him.

"Good morning, Mr. Briggs," Mr. Anderson greeted him. How do you like your new position now that you've been in it for a while?"

"Very much. I have to show my filing system to Franz. It should help him as he's on the area it was done for. Most of the team like it and are making their own, partly from mine. That's not why I sought this meeting."

"Oh, is there a problem?"

"Only a personal one. My fiancé has been here on a holiday and went home yesterday. I've to be here for a long time yet, so we're contemplating marriage and her coming to live here on a more permanent basis. What do you advise? Frau Wirth doesn't have married accommodation, but she has a friend who owns furnished flats where we could live."

"I'm willing to sanction the marriage and will help you to arrange time off. See this lady, and if you can get a decent place at a sensible price then go ahead. There's one point that you need to keep in mind. We'll be handing over to the Germans fairly soon. You shouldn't commit yourselves to a long term tenancy. If you sign up for one and a half years and then have to move on in six months you would lose money. Keep it on as flexible terms as possible.

"Whilst we are talking about these matters I'll bring up something else. When the German Government takes over some of the power here they will handle logistical problems, as we do now. They've said that they would like three of our people to stay on in their employ for at least a year, possibly longer. We've been doing the job and know the problems; they want a smooth transition.

"Would you be interested in one of those positions? You would be employed by them just as you are with us, yet overall you are British Government property until your three years are completed, or they shorten it. You would also remain on the Company's list of employees on loan, that means that when your contract with the Germans finishes you would be eligible for a post with us at a similar rate of salary as you receive from the Germans when you leave them. They are offering a high salary, much higher than you are receiving now."

"Nancy told me of this, but only as a possibility. Yes, I'm very interested. My father was three years unemployed for no fault of his own. We grew up in abject poverty. I don't worship money, but I want to obtain a very good reserve whilst I'm young to cover any future disaster. What are the chances of me obtaining one of these advisory posts?"

"I would expect you to get it. For South Germany I've been asked to nominate someone. As you want it your name will go forward. You are the best speaker of both German and French who's been in this office since I came here. You'll have to go before a German or perhaps several, but it's almost certain that you'll get it. If you're married and she's living here with you that should add weight to your claim. You may have to move to another part of the country, perhaps Bonn which will be the seat of the government as Berlin is out of the question at present. That's why I warned against long term agreements."

"That would be no problem as we've no relatives in either Munich or Bonn. Thank you for your support."

"You've earned it. When you marry you'll want to do it where your families are."

"Yes."

"I'll arrange time off when you give me the date."

"Thank you. Can that include a week over here as well?"

"I think so."

"There's one other small matter I hope to be able to resolve. Alice would like to have some kind of part-time work once we get settled in. She doesn't want long days of idleness. If you know of any possible ideas I'd like to hear them. Even unpaid charity work would be better than nothing. She has some German, but not like mine."

"I'll be able to find her something. When she's ready I'll solve her problem."

"Thank you again."

The following Saturday afternoon George went to see the friend of Frau Wirth. She said that she had a flat coming empty in three weeks, but before she re-let it there was work needed that would also call for some re-decorating, so it would probably be five weeks before it was ready. She told him the terms, and he explained that he wasn't his own master. They probably would wish to stay longer, but he might have to move to another city, so he didn't wish to commit himself to more than six months at a time. As he'd been sent by Frau Wirth she was agreeable to that, and she showed him a flat that was about to have a new occupant.

"They are all more or less on the same model as this one," she said.

"That will be satisfactory, Frau Wirth said that you would almost certainly have what we'd need."

Next day George wrote a long letter and posted it for the first collection on Monday. He telephoned Alice a few days later.

"Did you get my letter, darling?"

"Yes, it sounds just right for us. Mum and Dad say it seems alright, and if your Mr. Anderson says it will be I want us to go ahead. He should know the situation after all the time he's been over there."

"Very good, so now you'll have to do some organising as I'm stuck here. I can be there a few days before the wedding, but I can't ask too much of the boss. See the minister where Helen was married, and find a date for us after the flat is ready in five weeks.

"Then ask Dad to get Nigel to organise a reception in the restaurant on the Saturday afternoon after the ceremony. We only had part of it for Helen's, but we may have more guests so tell him the number and leave it to him and Sheila. We'll need our four including me, two Mouldings, four Donovans and Doris and her mother. I would like to invite Bob and Nancy, so please send them a card."

"I'll sleep at Mum's until we wed, but we'll need a room for two on the wedding night and the one after it. We'll fly to Germany on the Monday and we've the rest of that week as a honeymoon in the north of the country. We'll see plenty of birds up there. Get the date, and give us time to arrange cover for my absence. Mr. Anderson is being very helpful, so I want to leave things tidy for him. I'll telephone again next Sunday; can you get Mum or Dad there for 10.30 your time?"

"Yes, I'll do all of that, dear. You're a slave driver, sitting in your office issuing orders to your agents and your lady."

"Someone has to do the organising, but unfortunately I haven't learned how to be in two places at once, so I've to hope that you lot will do it right. Get Richard to see the minister if you like, he knows him. I'm glad that we were at Helen's wedding. It's the only one I ever attended. It's given me some idea of what we have to organise. Your parents will be able to advise if you cannot manage it all yourself."

+ + +

"I've both of your parents here," Alice said. "I'll let them speak to you first."

"Hello, George. So you're going to become a married man. Your dad is here, and he wants to tell you something. How are you?"

"I'm fine, Mum. How are all of you?"

"We're very well and very excited for you. Alice is here so I can't say much or she'll blush, but she's the right girl for you. Now I must let your dad talk to you."

"Hello, son. It's alright for you. Alice says that you have a fancy office from where you send out your commands. I'm glad to see that my son is so clever. Richard has booked the chapel and Alice will give you the details. I've booked the reception and the room for two nights. I've also booked another room for your friends at Manchester, but it's only for one night. Alice's mother and Sheila will sort out the Reception and the numbers. Sheila has ordered the cake from the people who made Helen's. Alec has volunteered to be Best Man if you've no other ideas."

"He's read my thoughts."

"He thought he should offer as you're so far away. Doris will be bridesmaid again."

"Can you arrange something with the dance promoter, or get Richard to do it?"

"I'll talk with Richard and we'll arrange something. Now there's a frantic woman here wanting me off the line, so here she is. Goodbye, son."

"What a job this getting married is. You'll have to be good to me after all this work."

"I will be. The flat is ours, and Frau Wirth will go in on the Monday to get it ready for us, putting in a bit of food and a drop of milk."

"In that case all I've to do is wait for the day and hope I'll have a bridegroom. We have the licence and the minister."

"Don't worry, the bridegroom will be there early to check that his staff have organised things properly."

Mr. Anderson knew people in North Germany and he found a good base for the honeymoon. "I chose Hamburg because it's close to the coast and the wild life that you want to see, but away from the crowds of tourists. Robert and Nancy will be envious of you."

Now all was ready and George booked his flight to Manchester. Alice was to collect him from there and both were eager for that to happen.

CHAPTER 15

The date for the wedding had been set for the second Saturday in June. Mr. Anderson agreed to George having two weeks away from his work, the first would be in England, and the second would be for a honeymoon in Germany. He flew to Manchester on the Saturday afternoon, a full week before the wedding.

It was one of the shortest weeks George had ever known. Plans were discussed and a visit to the little chapel and a meeting with the minister had to be arranged. Alice's wedding dress and the one for the bridesmaid arrived and had to be tried on to ensure all was well. George spent part of the week with his family and as much time as possible with Alice.

The important day arrived and the clock showed 1.30 as George and his brother walked up the lanes to the chapel. The sun was shining and they noticed that several farmers were working with their hay. Harry and Sarah Driver were taking a short break to watch the wedding. George was rather nervous as he stood waiting with Alec.

"Have you got the ring, Alec?"

"Of course I have. Calm down, George, this is a minister, not a monster, and you know that Alice is harmless."

After what had seemed an age to George Alice appeared at his side. She was accompanied by her father and Doris. In George's eyes she looked angelic. She was slightly taller than he was, and as he looked he saw her beautiful face hidden behind her veil. Because she was tall a long dress had been chosen with a flowing skirt that spread out from her body as it neared the ground. The veil had been designed in an older fashion, and that material also reached nearly to the floor.

Doris was wearing a dress similar in colour to the one she wore at Helen's wedding. It too was quite long and its pastel shade of yellow was perfect for her hair colour and looked well with the white of the bride. She carried a small posy of pink roses of matching shade to the larger bouquet in Alice's hand.

The ceremony was completed without any problem, and as Alec passed the ring to his brother he gave a smile as if to say, 'See, George, I didn't lose it.' It didn't take long for all the guests to arrive at the restaurant. George was very happy and Alice was almost speechless with delight.

"Darling, am I dreaming?" George asked as they awaited the first of their guests. "Are you really mine at last, or will I waken up and find myself in Munich and all this hasn't happened?"

"No, dear, you aren't dreaming. I'm your very happy bride. What I've wanted for a very long time has happened. Here come your father and mother."

It was some time before they again had time for a private word. George's parents were closely followed by Walter and Edith, and then the Drivers came behind them.

"Eh lad, this is a fine thing for you. When you used to help my sister with the hens we didn't expect such good things for you. I know that at present you're having to live abroad, but I hear that you're doing well. We both wish you and Alice a long and happy married life. Now we can't stay any longer; the field by the lane will be dry enough to take in now."

"Thanks for coming, Harry, and you too, Sarah. I'm sorry, but I can't come and help you today. I'm a bit busy," he added with a smile.

The farmer and his sister laughed as they departed to continue their own lives. Behind the families and friends Nigel and Sheila came to wish the happy couple well and check that all was as it should be as the people made their way to those tables that were prepared for them. Sheila had already ensured that the meal would be ready and perfectly prepared; now she wanted to supervise the serving of it.

All enjoyed the food, and the champagne was properly chilled and ready for the toasts. Seamus and Sean were too young for alcohol, so there was fruit juice of their choice for them to drink. The cake was a two tier delight. It had been decorated with several birds made of marzipan and icing sugar.

"Oh, George, this is too beautiful to cut," Alice said.

"Now dear, you mustn't talk nonsense. This is top quality fruit cake, and like Richard's cousin you know that I love it." He brandished the knife, "Come, help me to start the process whereby I can devour some of it."

"Surely you aren't hungry after that meal?"

"Only for fruit cake. Come on, let us cut."

Whilst all were being served the cake Ernest began the toasting.

"Ladies and Gentlemen, my sister has given me the job of getting you all to start drinking, but not too much. I have a word of warning for Sean and Seamus. Boys, don't ever let anyone persuade you to have a sister. They are a lot of bother when they find jobs for you to do. Mine told me I had to be toastmaster today. Really she's not too bad. George thinks that she's nice and I know he's right. He's got himself a really good wife today. Of course she's picked a very nice man as well. We wish them both a long and happy life together. Let's all drink to their health and prosperity."

George thanked him and expressed his pleasure because for the first time he had met Ernest's wife. Then William was called on to speak.

"I'm not a trained speaker, folks, but I know when I'm happy. Today I've seen my elder son marry the loveliest woman after my Gwen in this part of Yorkshire. I wish to call for a toast for the parents who raised her."

Walter responded, "Thank you, William. We know our Alice, and she's a wise girl. She would never marry a man who didn't have good parents. Let us drink to the health of Gwen and William."

Now Ernest called on Alec who arose to his feet. "Well, everyone, I don't think that you want to hear me for long. Our George is the man of the day, but there is one thing I want to say. Ernest warned the boys about sisters, well I'll let you into a secret, older brothers are no better. Mine found me this Best Man job. That's not really true. In a weak moment I thought that as he was away I should offer to help, but I expected him to say he had someone else in mind. He didn't, and I was stuck, but there's one good side to it, I did manage to get him wed without him making a mess of it.

"Also it gives me the chance to say what a lovely bridesmaid we had. I want to ask you all to drink to the health of Miss Doris Slater. Now, Doris, I wasn't here when you were a bridesmaid before, but I heard about it. I heard that Mr. Moulding's brother danced with you afterwards, and that you dance very well. Now, if you were willing to dance with a man from Devonshire is there a chance that I could have one tonight?"

"I think there may be," the blushing young lady said with a smile.

The party had passes for the dance, so when it started they all went down to the hall. Many of the dancers didn't know Alice and George very well, but most knew William. Some had seen the newlyweds when the Mouldings married, and on other rare visits. Quite a few came across to wish them well. Alice had entered the hall in her wedding dress, but shortly afterwards she went up to the room they had hired to change into more practical clothes. Several thanked her for letting them see the dress.

Alec got his dance with Doris who by this time was a very good dancer. The men made sure that Gladys wasn't short of partners, and the widow really enjoyed the evening. The dance didn't end until eleven o'clock, but George and Alice left before ten. They were rather tired, and felt a need to be by themselves. They had been waiting for this all evening.

After the week of preparation they enjoyed the quiet of the Sunday. After a late breakfast they spent the morning in their room before walking down into the valley. Gwen was delighted to be able to feed her son and his wife a good Sunday dinner before they left. They stayed some time after it, then farewells were said as they would be leaving early on the Monday.

Before going to Alice's old home they walked down to the hide and had a last look at the dam. When they came to England again Alice's parents would be living in Cullerton and the dam would belong to another. They watched several young mallards and coots for about half an hour.

"Come on, George, we must go to Mum and Dad," Alice said. "Dad will see us tomorrow when he takes us to Manchester, but this will be the last time for Mum, and it'll be a long while before she sees me again."

"Yes, I may not get away for many months, but of course you could pop over to see them occasionally."

They were greeted at the house with a mixture of happiness and sadness. Edith was preparing to lose her daughter to a foreign land for an unknown period. Overall the time was very pleasant and George really felt that he'd been accepted into the family. He thought how lucky he was after the poverty of his childhood. Now he was married to the only woman who had ever interested him, and she was the daughter of the local mill owner.

Walter wouldn't be a mill owner much longer. He'd come to an agreement with Peter Greenwood who owned the next mill upstream that he would take over the mill as a going concern and keep the employees in work. Walter and Edith had bought a nice bungalow in the village, with enough room for their daughter and George to stay when they wished.

Next morning Walter was at the hotel very early to take the young couple to catch their aeroplane. It left the ground exactly on time and they had a comfortable flight to Munich where they landed safely. Mr. Anderson had sent Eileen with the car to collect them.

"I seem to be gradually developing into your personal chauffeur," Eileen remarked with a smile.

"That's because you're such a good driver," George told her. "I'm certainly grateful for your help. It's a great comfort to me when I know that the car is safely locked in the garage whilst I'm away. Unfortunately I fear that your services won't be required again for a long time, if ever. You may even have gone home before I get another chance to go over again."

Eileen rode in the back as George drove and Alice sat beside him. When they had dropped her at the office George drove to the flat, and he was relieved when Alice said she liked the place he'd obtained for them to use as home. Frau Wirth had kept her promise, and there were enough provisions for them before they left for the north next morning. There was an envelope propped next to the teapot and inside it George found the name and address of the hotel where they would stay in Hamburg.

"Have you been to Hamburg?" Alice asked.

"No, but Mr. Anderson says it will be interesting for us. It's a very important port and was bombed heavily in the war. It's the birthplace of both Brahms and Mendelssohn, so there will probably be an interesting museum if we want some indoor activity on a wet day. It's in the north German plain and some parts are said to be very beautiful, but the city has a lot of industry. This week it'll be the home of the loveliest girl in the world."

"And the nicest man. How far have we to go?"

"I think it's about four hundred miles. I don't use the autobahn unless I have to do, so it'll probably take all day. I'll drive until we stop for refreshments, then you can take over and practice your left-hand driving. After lunch I'll take over again and maybe you'll finish the journey."

"Why don't you use the autobahn?"

"Johann took me on it one Sunday morning when it was very quiet and I did reasonably well, but he advised me to avoid it when I could until I got used to German roads. I can use it now without difficulty, but I prefer not to do so."

"It seems he was a good teacher."

"Yes, I've arranged for him to take you out a couple of times when we get back. Today you'll be on good roads and city by-passes. He'll help you to get used to city driving, and he may take you on the autobahn. The main things you've to get used to are a car that is wrong way around for us, and driving on the right."

As most drivers sought the very fast roads those George used were reasonably quiet and they could make good progress. Alice was able to see some fine scenery. George had reckoned eight hours for driving and two for the breaks. They left the flat at eight o'clock and he hoped to be at the hotel by around six. He wasn't far wrong as they pulled into its car park at 6.30.

A quick wash soon refreshed them and they went down to dinner both hungry and happy. After the meal they went for a short stroll along the bank of the Elbe. It was a pleasant evening and the fresh air after a days travel made them feel rather weary, so they soon went in and retired to their room.

Mr. Anderson had chosen their base well. During the week they visited several places of interest including a museum dedicated to the two famous composers, but having other interesting things as well. They spent one day on the coast and saw several seabird colonies and other things of interest. Of most importance to them was the fact that they were together again and would remain so. After their long separation it seemed wonderful to be able to spend both day and night in each other's company. Of course all good things come to an end, and Saturday arrived all too soon.

"Now, George, I want to go shopping today," Alice told her husband. "When we get back to Munich tomorrow I want to be a good wife and have something to feed you. We'll have to get our Sunday dinner at a hotel on the way home, but we'll need some more food before the shops open on Monday."

They spent some time exploring the shopping section of the city, then used the remainder of the day to rest and enjoy being together before the long journey next day.

George returned to the office on the Monday, and once he had satisfied the curiosity of the others as far as he wished to go life continued as he knew it. At the end of the day it seemed too good to be true. Unless it was raining, or at the weekend, he left the car in the company garage and got some exercise walking the short distance to their home. As he approached the flat Alice was looking out for him, and she usually met him at the door. They would spend a few minutes together and then she would produce a well cooked meal. Most evenings were spent at home, and they had other interests to share as well as wild life. Both were avid readers and Alice enjoyed various kinds of needlework. She knitted clothes for both herself and George as well as things for a charity where she spent some of her time.

At weekends, if the weather was suitable, George took her to various lakes and other beauty spots he'd found in the time he'd worked in the state. Sometimes he had to go to one of his agents, and he would try to arrange the meeting for the Monday. They would then leave home on the Saturday afternoon and spend all of Sunday exploring the area.

Working for a charity helped Alice to widen her vocabulary and she even made a few female friends from it. After a while she limited her time there to one day each week. She didn't want to lose her typing and other skills she'd learned at school and in her father's office.

Mr Anderson found her work in the office two days each week and she was able to get the practice she wanted. Most of her work was on an English machine, doing things to go to Head Office, but she also began to use the German machine with a different keyboard. One day, about six months after the wedding, Mr. Anderson called them both into his office. As is normal on such occasions they both were apprehensive. Had one of them done something terribly wrong?

"Good morning, Mr. and Mrs. Briggs," he greeted them with a smile that allayed their fears. "The time has come of which I spoke before you were married. Are you still interested in working for the German Government, George?"

"If things are going to be as you expected them to be the answer is 'Yes.'"

"They seem to be. How do you feel about it, Mrs. Briggs?"

"As he still has to be British Government property for over a year we may as well work for the Germans as anyone else. If he turns it down we could end up anywhere."

"I feel that you are both thinking in the right way. As you still want the job you'll have to make the journey to Frankfurt-am-Main. The Government will be in Bonn, but the work you do will be controlled from Frankfurt. I'll contact their people and make an appointment for you to see someone about the situation, and make another recommendation for you. It seems that they've decided that they only need two of you instead of three.

"You'll be given details there of what's required, and as there will only be two of you for the whole of the country I would expect the salary to be increased accordingly. I recommend that you both go to the interview. If they see and talk with you, Mrs. Briggs, they'll see that you're not the unreliable type who could make the husband unsuitable. I'll let you know the details of the appointment as soon as I have them."

Later that day he told George they were to be at an office in Frankfurt at noon on the following Monday. As this would mean about four hours of driving they decided to go on the Saturday afternoon. Mr. Anderson found a hotel for them to use, and told George to bring the receipted bill to him.

By this time it was late January and they ran into snow after about a hundred miles of driving. It wasn't heavy, but they had to slow down somewhat. This was compensated for to some extent by the beauty of the snow on the hills and trees as they passed. The hotel was a good one, and they spent most of Sunday there as it was pointless to go exploring strange country in such wintry conditions.

On Monday they arrived at the meeting place in good time for the interview. After a short wait they were ushered into a room where a tall dark haired man aged about fifty was waiting for them.

"Good morning, Herr and Frau Briggs. I am pleased that you have come together because I like to see what the wife is like. If the wife is good the husband may be. If she is not we have no hope."

Alice was dressed in a well cut woollen costume in a very dark green colour. It was warm and suited her young features. They all spoke generally about the weather and the journey for a few minutes.

"So you didn't come to Frankfurt today?"

"No, we came on Saturday afternoon. We had no snow in Munich and were hoping to see a little of this part of Germany and its wild life, but when we saw the snow we decided to stay indoors most of the time.

"You are interested in the birds?"

"Yes, we both are, and also the other creatures. I've never been in this part before, so both my wife and I hoped to see something new to us."

"In that case you won't be bored if you have to live here for a long time?"

"I don't think so. I've already been in your country for over one and a half years and I've never been bored. Of course we would prefer to be nearer to our families, but as we can't we may as well use the time to learn about the places where we are."

"How do you feel about it, Frau Briggs? Will you be happy if you live here for two years or more?"

"Where my husband is I'll be happy," she replied.

"Your Herr Anderson has recommended you. Certainly your German is very good, nearly as good as mine and I was born here. Let me tell you what we would want you to do, and what you would be paid. We want a smooth transition as we take over the affairs your people have been handling since the war ended. You and one Frenchman are considered the right people to work with us to obtain that smoothness."

He spoke for about twenty minutes and occasionally fired a question to George. Mr. Anderson had given George a large sealed envelope to give to the German whose name was Herr Heine. At this point he opened the envelope and studied its contents for a few minutes.

"Herr Briggs, am I to believe what Herr Anderson has written here?"

"I don't know what is in that document, but whatever he wrote will be the truth. He's a good man."

"That's what he says about you and your wife. You will come to live in Frankfurt and start work here in this building on the first Monday in March at nine o'clock in the morning. Unless we find you useless and have to sack you the contract will be for two years, twenty-four months. We may ask you to stay longer, but that is for the future to decide. Should I tell you what your salary will be when your wife is listening?"

"We have no secrets from each other," George told him.

The figure that Herr Heine mentioned as a starting salary made it difficult for Alice to hide her amazement. It was clear that George's services were really wanted. The German then produced a legal agreement for George to sign.

"You may need to take it and read it at your own speed. I don't know how quickly you can read our language, but I would like it signed as soon as possible."

"I probably will read it as fast as you would, and understand what I read. I read and think in German without having to translate. We will read it now, and I'll sign before we leave if it is as it should be."

"Then I will leave you for a while so that you can read it together. Will one hour be long enough or will you need longer?"

"I won't need so long, but my wife is not as fluent so an hour will be about right."

The German left them, and a few minutes later a young girl entered with two cups of coffee, cream, sugar and a selection of small cakes. She left immediately and they settled down to read. Alice occasionally had to ask George to translate a word, but she was able to read and understand most of it.

"This is amazing. The money they are offering is more than Dad got out of the mill in the last two years. He had to lay out capital and risk the wool market as well. I know, because I saw the figures when I was in the mill office. That was what made him think it was time to retire."

"Do you agree that I should take it?" George asked when they had read it and thoroughly discussed the offer.

"If you feel its right then do it. Sign the paper if you'll be happy here for two years. It's too good to miss, and it's only a few months more than your service to our Government has to be."

When Herr Heine returned George handed him the document.

"Welcome to our team," the German said. We will look forward to seeing you in March."

George and Alice found that the two years at Frankfurt sped by very quickly. They were very happy in the marriage. She came home to England after the first year and stayed a month. Two of the Sundays were spent with the Briggs family.

From their flat in Frankfurt they were able to visit many beautiful places that would have been too far away when they were in Munich. The Germans were more than satisfied with the help they got from George, and at the end of the two years Herr Heine called him into his office.

"Herr Briggs, your contract is coming to its end. Your help has been invaluable; the filing system you set up for us is working well. If you would like to stay here we'll be very happy to give you another post where you can help us. We'll increase your pay, and there will be further opportunities in the future. What do you think, Herr Briggs?"

"It sounds very good, and I've enjoyed working with you all. If I only had myself to please I would probably accept your offer immediately, but I've a wife and we both have families in England. Before I say one way or the other I want to discuss it with Frau Briggs."

"That is sensible. If you stay or you go you both need to be happy, and it's right that you remember your parents. Go home and talk to your wife, then tell me what you have decided."

"Thank you for the offer, whether we accept or not I appreciate it."

When George arrived at the flat Alice had the meal ready to eat so he didn't mention Herr Heine until later in the evening.

"It's a wonderful offer, and I don't mind staying longer if you don't. The money is amazing."

"Yes, dear, they realise that you are special. We should be satisfied with what we've had. I think it is time to go home. You see, I believe that our parents would want their first grandchild to be born in Yorkshire, and the doctor says he or she will be with us before next winter."

THE END

Part of UKUnpublished.co.uk   .CO.UK

UKBookland gives you the opportunity to purchase all of the books published by UKUnpublished.

Do you want to find out a bit more about your favourite UKUnpublished Author?

Find other books they have written?

PLUS – UKBookland offers all the books at Excellent Discounts to the Recommended Retail Price!

You can find UKBookland at www.ukbookland.co.uk

Find out more about **Mervyn S. Whale** and his books.

Are you an Author?

Do you want to see your book in print?

Please look at the UKUnpublished website:
www.ukunpublished.co.uk

Let the World Share Your Imagination

Lightning Source UK Ltd.
Milton Keynes UK
07 October 2010

160893UK00001B/17/P